Always and Forever

Happy Reading!

Cathe Swanson

The Glory Quilts Series
Book 1

Cathe Swanson

www.catheswanson.com

ISBN-13: 978-1-949412-10-9

This is a work of fiction. Names, characters, businesses, places, events, locales, and incidents are either the products of the author's imagination or used in a fictitious manner. Any resemblance to actual persons, living or dead, or actual events is purely coincidental.

Connect with me online:

Twitter: https://twitter.com/catheswanson

Instagram: https://instagram.com/catheswanson

Pinterest: http://pinterest.com/catheswanson

Facebook: https://www.facebook.com/catheswanson

Scripture quotations are from the ESV® Bible (The Holy Bible, English Standard Version®), copyright © 2001 by Crossway, a publishing ministry of Good News Publishers. Used by permission. All rights reserved.

Dedication

This one is for my sweet daughter-in-law, Jennie Timmons, who has been my #1 cheerleader since I embarked on this writing career. She encourages me and holds me accountable—and she always laughs at the funny parts!

1

Next year, with new trees and green grass, the house would be perfect. Penny Anderson looked beyond the weeds and tree stumps to her new home. Her studio. Her place of business. The old farmhouse, so dirty and dilapidated just six months ago, had been transformed by new windows and gray paint into something more dignified. The only other exterior change had been the front porch with wide steps, to welcome visitors—clients—and the blue door, to invite them inside.

The blue door was open. Penny cradled a bolt of fabric as she mounted the stairs. She could hear tinny music, but no power tools or hammers indicated the presence of workmen. Maybe someone was painting and cracked the door open for fresh air. She shifted her bundle to one arm and stepped onto the threshold, turning sideways to bump the door open with her hip.

The door rebounded on her, and she staggered back. Something clattered on the other side of the door, and Penny looked up at a muffled shout of pain and ducked her head just in time to protect her face from the coil of wire spilling down on her. She pushed it off and held out the fabric to examine it for damage.

"Don't you know how to knock?"

"I didn't know you were back there. Are you all

right?" Penny moved forward again, peering up at the man who glowered at her over the top of the door.

"No. The door slammed into my face and nearly knocked me off the ladder." He leaned forward and stuck out his hand. "I need the wire back."

"Are you—" Penny came to a horrified stop as something red splashed onto the white satin in her arms. The stain bloomed on the heavy fabric. More blood fell, and Penny shrieked as she jumped away. "You're bleeding!"

"You got my nose with—"

"Stop it!"

"Stop bleeding?" The man disappeared and then opened the door, dragging a step ladder behind him. "Penny?" He stared at the brilliant splotches on the white fabric. "Sorry!" He pushed his hand against his nose. The blood had already dripped into his blond beard.

Penny whirled to face the road. No car. Aunt Violet would be halfway home by now, and she wouldn't answer her phone while she was driving.

She pushed past the man, nearly tripping over his tools in her haste. In the workroom, she set the bolt on the table and pulled back the top layer. The blood had penetrated the folds of heavy silk.

"This stuff cost fifty dollars a yard!"

"Is it bad?" He still held his nose in both hands, obscuring most of his face. What she could see was bloody.

"Do you have arteries in your nose?"

He ignored that. "Can I help you wash it?"

"It can't be washed. It has to be dry cleaned, and I

don't have a car to drive into town. Just stay back." She sounded like a shrew, but it wasn't as if it was a real injury. The stupid man had a bloody nose. She continued to unfold the fabric, mentally assessing the damage in dollars and cents. There was no way she could cut around this much blood.

"I'll drive you. My truck is out back."

His truck was probably filthy, and there was no way she was getting in a truck with a stranger.

"No, thank you."

Something in his eyes made her pause. Despite his remorse, he looked almost amused. He regarded her, as if waiting. Recognition dawned.

"Brian?"

He nodded, still holding his nose. "Welcome home."

But he was the one who had been gone. Penny wrapped the fabric back around the bolt. "Let's go." She strode toward the back door without waiting for him.

"I'll lock up."

"Fine."

He caught up with her at the truck. It was just a blue pickup, not a work truck, and relatively clean. Brian unlocked the door with a fob and reached out to open it for her. Penny gasped as blood streamed over his beard. His nose was swollen.

"Is it broken?"

"Maybe." He ran his fingers over it, and they came away bloody.

"I'll drive." She reached for the fob and snatched her hand back.

Brian glanced at the fob, wiped it on his jeans and held it out.

"But… your fabric." He nodded at the bulky parcel. "You can't hold it while you drive. And I…"

"You're a bloody mess," she snapped. "I'm dropping this off at the cleaners and then I'll take you to the hospital."

"No, no." It came out with d's instead of n's. She walked around the truck and climbed in the driver's side, settling the fabric on her lap.

"It won't work," Brian said. "You'll have to move the seat forward."

Was he enjoying himself? Penny growled in frustration. She set the bolt of fabric on the seat between them. "Don't touch it." It was rude, but she didn't have time for the niceties.

"I'll bleed in the other direction."

She turned the key. The truck lurched forward and stalled. Penny instinctively stomped on the clutch, but it was too late. She whipped her head around at Brian's protesting yelp.

"A manual transmission? Really?"

"Do you know how to drive—"

"Yes, of course I know how to drive a clutch. I just wasn't expecting it." She adjusted the fabric so she could reach the gear shift and restarted the engine, hoping her rusty skills wouldn't embarrass her.

She sneaked a peek at Brian. He leaned back against the seat with his head tipped back, both hands covering his face. She should have recognized him, even with the long hair and beard. Was his nose really broken?

"Are you okay?"

"Yeah." He lifted his left hand to look at her. "I'm sorry about your fabric."

She grunted, keeping her eyes on the road. It wasn't his fault. "I'm sorry about your face."

He chuckled. "That sounds like a junior high insult."

"How would you know? You never went to junior high," Penny scoffed.

"I might have said it to my sisters. When Mom wasn't around, of course. That was a drawback of homeschooling. There were so few opportunities to harass girls."

"I'm sure you picked it right up when you went to college." Of course, he'd probably not wanted to harass the girls there. "My brothers found plenty of opportunities to tease me. Still do."

"I heard Jeremy and Nicole have a baby now."

"She's a year old," Penny said, "and cute as a bug. A real ham."

"Your sister Sarah—You call her Sadie, right? — she's the same age as Angel. I've heard all about her. And Mark and Lisa are both away at college? Faith said Mark was planning to go to medical school."

"Faith didn't tell me you were coming home." Brian's sister was her best friend. Why hadn't she mentioned it?

"She didn't know." His voice was as smug as it could be under the circumstances. "I surprised them all."

"How long are you staying?" Penny brought the car to a stop at the intersection, praying she could get it moving again without jerking them around.

"Forever. I've got a job in Princeton."

"Really?" Penny turned to look at him. "You surprised them with that? I bet your mom's thrilled."

"Mostly. We're still adjusting. I made arrangements for an apartment in Princeton, but Dad wants me to stay with them while I get my house built, to save money." He shrugged. "We'll see how it goes. It was a little awkward this morning, when I had to tell Mom I'm not going to church with them tomorrow. She's not very happy."

"You're not going to church?"

"I'm going to Riverdale with Faith and Jim."

"Oh." No wonder Brian's mother was unhappy. She'd already lost a daughter to a church she didn't approve of. It didn't matter to her that the doctrine was nearly identical to her own. It was all about the externals for Mrs. Michaels.

"Do you still go there, too?" Brian asked.

"Oh, yeah. We all do." She glanced at him. Were his eyes swelling up? Maybe she should take him to the hospital before going to the dry cleaners.

"You'll be there tomorrow?"

"Yes," Penny said. "I'm planning on it."

"Good. I'm going to blame you for my broken nose."

He did blame her, too. Penny watched with indignation as Brian, in conversation across the room, gestured in her direction. At least his friends looked entertained instead of shocked or censorious. It wasn't her fault. She couldn't have known someone was standing on a ladder right behind the front door. He should have made some noise or something. Hung a sign on the door.

Her father should be taking his share of the blame, too, since he'd made the arrangements without letting her know someone would be there on Saturday. Monday would have been fine. She didn't even want a stupid exit sign. At least it wasn't bright red. The green was inconspicuous in comparison.

"Were you surprised to see Brian?"

"Hi!" Penny hugged Faith. "I sure was. That's how he ended up with a broken nose."

"Serves him right," said Brian's sister. "It sounds like he was hiding behind the door. How were you supposed to know?"

"And now he's telling everyone I broke his nose!"

"No, he's telling everyone he bled all over five hundred dollars' worth of silk fabric because he was leaning over the door to see what a pretty girl you'd grown up to be." Faith chuckled.

"He's seen me several times since I've grown up," Penny said, "and never commented on that before. And he didn't mention it yesterday."

"Did the blood come out of the fabric?"

"I don't know yet. Pray that it does, because Brian chose to bleed all over the most expensive piece I've ever bought. I don't think it would be covered by insurance."

"Oh, come on. He didn't do it on purpose."

Penny sighed. "No, he didn't. It really was my

fault. The door was open a crack, and I could hear music inside, so I knew someone was there. I just didn't know he was behind the door when I shoved it open."

"It was an accident," Faith said, "and hopefully the fabric will wash up just fine."

"That's the other thing," Penny said. "I shouldn't have brought that fabric over there at all. It's a construction zone! But I wanted to see how it looked under the new lights, and I'm getting impatient. I want to start bringing everything over and getting it organized."

"When will you be ready for that?"

"Soon, I hope. I want to move in on January first. I'd like to start working over there within the next couple of weeks, but I can't have wedding gowns smelling of paint fumes, and I keep changing the layout of the workroom."

"Let me know if I can help with anything," Faith said. She watched her daughter advancing on them. "What do you want to bet Angel's going to ask if she can go over to your house today?"

"Sadie got a new game. She's been stomping us all week, so I'd be happy to bring her a new victim—er, new competitor."

"Hi, Aunt Penny." The girl turned to her mother. "Can I go to Sadie's house today? Her mom said it's okay."

"Yes, you can." Faith flipped her daughter's ponytail. "Do you want to go home and change first?"

"No, I'm fine. If I need something, I can borrow it from Sadie." She ran off, weaving around people and scooting along the pews where the aisle was blocked.

"They remind me of us at that age," Penny said. "I'm glad they have each other."

"Me, too, and now that you have her for the rest of the day, I think I'll go out to lunch with my husband. He's around here somewhere."

Penny pointed. "Aunt Violet has him backed into a corner. She wants some senior citizen cushions for the pews. Something thick, to make it easier to stand up. Ever since she sprained her ankle and was in a wheelchair for a week, she's an expert on accessibility."

"It's a good idea," Faith said, "but let's go rescue him. I'm hungry, and you need to collect a couple of sugared-up eight-year-old girls. They're over there by the donuts. Good luck!"

"Has it occurred to you that Aunt Violet has some hoarding issues? Maybe from growing up during the depression or something?" Penny shoved a tote into the back of the Suburban. "Jeffrey said there's another thirty boxes in the basement."

"Possibly. She says it doesn't count as hoarding as long as it's neatly labeled and organized." Her mother grunted as she handed her the next box. "When she moved in with us, she wanted all this stuff right in her room, but eventually your Dad talked her into putting some of it downstairs."

"What's in here?" Penny squinted at the label. "It weighs a ton."

Her mother turned the box to read it. "I don't think

your aunt knows how to print. It says, 'foundation fabrics.' It must be for her family quilts. I think it's all for family quilts."

"How many quilts does she plan to make?"

"I don't know. As many as she can, I think, and she's probably planning to leave all of it to one of you girls to finish."

Penny grimaced. "Hopefully, Lisa or Adrienne. Or even Sadie."

"None of them sew like you do." Constance heaved another box into the truck and straightened to rub her back. "This is why I never took up sewing. Fabric is too heavy. It's a good thing you had your grandma to teach you."

"But I don't hoard fabric like Aunt Vi does. She's always asking for the remnants."

"For her quilts."

Penny backed out of the SUV and dropped onto a tote. "I really don't want to make quilts. I do wedding dresses."

"It's just one, isn't it? And she is giving you a house, after all."

"Not giving," Penny said, "but I know everyone's going to see it that way! It's more of a lease, or a slow transfer."

"I know." Constance squatted to read a label. "This is books, not fabric. I'll let Jeffrey lift it. You don't need to worry about what other people think."

"What about my aunts and uncles? I'm sure they don't think it's fair for me to inherit the house and they get nothing." Penny walked to the garage door to look for her brother. "That's probably how they see it."

"I don't think so. Besides, it's her house, and no one else wants to move in with her." Constance put an arm around her daughter. "By the time you pay for all the renovations, just to make it livable, the property taxes, utilities, maintenance, and everything else, you'll have bought that house outright. And you're letting Aunt Violet live there for the rest of her life. That's what she wanted. And there might come a time when you'll have expenses for her care, too."

"I know. She was pretty blunt about it. The contract is about a hundred pages long, and it covers every detail. She even had Mr. Breyerton read it to me with Dad there, to make sure I knew what I was signing."

"She's sharper than most people realize. You're not taking advantage of her in any way. She's coming out of this deal just fine."

2

"Are you putting up a sign?"

"I guess so." Penny turned to look at the front yard. "I need to hire a graphic designer to make me a logo."

"You're a designer," Brian said. "Can't you just design it yourself?"

"Not my skill set. All that branding stuff is a big deal." Penny gave a rueful chuckle. "I'm afraid of commitment."

"Branding? Like cows?"

"Like Nike and Disney and McDonalds. You see the swoosh and you immediately think running shoes. That's branding."

"Oh. Got it."

"I don't want to pick something in a hurry and hate it a year from now. But I'm supposed to be marketing the business before it even opens, and I can't do that without a logo, so..." She turned her palms up in a shrug. "I need to get one. Then I can put up a sign."

Brian dropped his tool belt on the floor and shut the door. "I suppose you have plenty to do already. Your dad said you needed the workroom wired for a few more irons."

"I don't think the electrician understood. I tried to explain it to him, but he's a friend of Dad's and still thinks

I'm eight years old and making doll clothes. He did it practically for free, so Dad doesn't want to ask him to fix it."

"No problem. I'm kind of between jobs right now."

"I thought you had a new job," Penny said.

"I do, but it keeps getting delayed."

He was probably glad for the work, even if his living expenses were low. Penny glanced at the ceiling. "I'd also like to change some of the lighting. I thought I liked what I had, but it was different after I painted."

Brian saluted. "Yes, ma'am."

"It's good to have you home. I'm sorry about your nose."

"What about the black eyes?" He blinked owlishly at her.

"That, too. It was a blanket apology. Does it hurt much?"

"No, not bad. I'm just glad I don't have to start my new job this week."

Penny winced. "They'd think you'd been in a fight. I am sorry. Not that it was my fault, with you hiding behind the door like that, but I'm sorry it happened."

Brian rolled his swollen eyes. At least, she thought he did. It was hard to tell.

"I have to make some business phone calls today." She hadn't meant to say that. Penny turned to leave, hoping he'd hear it as a farewell, not a conversation starter.

"Yeah? You don't sound enthusiastic."

"It was one of Dad's requirements for funding this. I have to jump into the business world with both feet and establish myself as a professional member of the business community."

He raised his brows. "What does he want you to do?"

"Chamber of commerce, small business counseling, lawyer, accountant... all of it."

"All at once, before you're even open?"

"Yep. You know Dad. He says I won't try as hard if I don't have skin in the game."

Brian cocked his head. "I think you would. You're not a quitter. But the principle's true for just about everything. And you'll get more respect if you do those things."

"I know. I don't want to look like a little old lady making dresses in her home." She scowled. "Or quilts. I don't do quilts."

"Why not? There's nothing wrong with making quilts. My mom does, and so does Faith."

"It's not me. I make dresses. Not crafts."

Penny lifted the handset a few inches and dropped it back on its base. Her desk, spotless amidst the construction clutter, held only the closed laptop and the telephone. Nothing to distract her from the business of... well, business. She blew out a sigh and started over, carefully tapping in the numbers. If she was going to be a professional businesswoman, she'd have to learn to do things like this.

Her call was answered on the first ring, before she

could lose her nerve and hang up again. "Mille Lacs Regional Chamber of Commerce. This is Maggie. How can I help you?"

"Hi. I'm interested in your Entrepreneur Mentorship Program. And joining the Chamber of Commerce, too." Lies, lies, lies. She wasn't at all interested, but she'd agreed to do it, along with Dad's other requirements, in exchange for cashing in the rest of her college savings to start her own business.

"We have the forms online, or you can pick them up here at the chamber office. Are you a new business?"

"Yes. I'm not technically open yet—not as a real business." Penny took a deep breath and reluctantly elaborated. "I've been working from home until now, but I'll be moving into my own shop soon."

"In the Mille Lacs area?"

"Yes, just north of Page."

After a few seconds of silence, Maggie repeated, "North of Page?"

"Yes." Penny bit back an array of comments ranging from sarcasm to justification. It was none of the woman's business. Or was it? She was asking for assistance and chamber membership, after all.

"It's a dressmaking business. Mostly bridal gowns."

"North of Page?"

The woman's disbelief annoyed Penny. "Yes!"

"Is this primarily an online business?"

"No, it turns out I can't make dresses on the computer. I have to use a sewing machine."

Another moment of silence. Penny refused to break

it.

"Okay," said the skeptical Maggie, "you can fill out the forms online or get them here." She rattled off the office hours and disconnected.

So much for being professional. She'd been rude and sarcastic—something that was happening more often lately. Penny leaned back in her chair and closed her eyes. "Oh, God, please help me."

A male sound—clearing his throat? —came from the doorway. "I know you weren't addressing me, but is there anything I can help with?"

Penny sat upright, horrified, and then relaxed at the sight of Brian. "You startled me." She nodded toward the phone. "I was just repenting of my 'compensatory snark'. Someone questioned my business choices, and I was rude to her. Maybe I should call her back and apologize."

"Really?" Brian raised one eyebrow. "She dared to question you?"

"Stop it. I know it sounds like a crazy idea, opening a shop way out here and expecting it to support me, but she kept repeating 'north of Page' as if it was on the moon. It's only ten minutes from town! We made it in eight on Saturday."

He shuddered dramatically. "Don't remind me. My nerves—and my truck—will never be the same again."

She narrowed her eyes and crossed her arms across her chest. "Did you need something or are you just bored?"

"Well," he stopped and regarded her thoughtfully.

"What?"

"I need to question your business choices."

"Why?" Penny raised an eyebrow right back at him. Better than him, as always.

"Your security system. Both of the locks have a five-digit entry code and then another one on the inside. I'm sure you could remember the codes, but the keypads are small, with letters and numbers. I don't want to install it if it's not what you want." He pulled a rectangular panel from his pocket and set it on her desk.

Penny looked at the keypad. Unlike a computer keyboard, the letters appeared to be in alphabetical order and the numbers were on the side instead of on top. She touched one of the buttons. Even in the bright light of her new office, the tiny characters shifted and leaned against one another. She squeezed her eyes shut, and when she opened them again, it was worse. She pushed it back toward Brian.

"No. That won't work."

He picked it up. "I saw a good four-digit deadbolt lock at the hardware store. I'll get two of them for the front and back doors."

"Thanks."

"No problem. I've got some things to pick up for myself." He paused in the doorway. "Did the blood come out of the fabric?"

Penny nodded. "All except for the first fold, and I can cut around that part. But I'm not bringing any more fabric over here until it's all cleaned up. I'll have to keep working at home."

"Your dad said you're still living at home."

"Just until it's all ready here." Penny looked around, seeing beyond the walls of her small office, imagining the finished house. "I can't wait."

"And your Aunt Violet's moving in with you?"

"Yes. It sounds like you and Dad had quite a chat!"

Brian shook his head. "That was about the sum of it. Just that you're opening a bridal shop in the old farmhouse and you and your aunt are going to live here. He said there were a few odd jobs to do, and would I be willing to help. I was. I am."

"I appreciate it. There are so many odd jobs. The house is in good condition, and the real renovations are all done, but I didn't even think about things like a security system or that stupid exit sign. It doesn't end."

"There's always something," Brian agreed. "It looks good so far, though, and if anyone can make a go of it, you can. Don't call that woman back. If you talk to her again, you can always apologize then, if you still want to. I think you overestimate the bite of your 'compensatory snark'." He grinned. "I'd forgotten about that term."

"You're the one who made it up! I've never forgotten it. It keeps me humble." She grinned back at him. "But only after I've been snarky and regretted it. It never occurs to me before I open my mouth."

"That's the trick. Think first, speak later. I think there's something in the Bible about that." He waved and left the office.

Penny watched him leave, wondering when her old friend—her best friend's younger brother—had grown into such a confident man. He'd been scrawny and insecure, not much taller than she was, when he left.

They'd all expected Brian to attend their denomination's college in St. Paul and become a pastor or missionary. But then he left—away to an engineering school in another state, a week after Faith's wedding. Penny was left behind, confused, missing both her friends.

And now Brian was back—different, but still Brian. He'd realized she might have a problem with the security system, and he took care of it. He'd always been good that way, accepting her for who she was. He didn't pretend her dyslexia didn't exist, but he didn't make a big deal of it. She'd forgotten how comfortable he was.

3

I can't believe it's the same place." Violet Anderson opened the car door but didn't step out. "It surprises me every time I see it. Gray and white with a blue door, instead of all white. And the porch. The boys built a porch once, from wood when a neighbor's house was demolished. It didn't hold up well."

"Dad built this one. It'll last forever. I like the way it looks with the wide steps." Penny held out her hand to assist her aunt. "Maybe we'll put some chairs up there so we can sit outside."

"We sat out back, where we had shade and a nicer view." Violet looped her cane over her arm and held the handrail to climb the stairs.

Penny glanced behind them. The house faced the road, across from hundreds of flat acres of ripening soybeans, broken by rows and clumps of windbreak trees. "You have a nice view out front, and only woods behind you."

"It was more open back then. Before all the trees grew up, we could see the river from here."

"Really? That would be nice." Penny recited the code aloud as she tapped on the lock and was pleased when the door opened on her first attempt. "Are you ready to see it? Close your eyes."

She held her aunt's elbow as Violet walked

through the doorway and came to a stop. "Open your eyes!" She watched, gleeful and anxious, as the older woman surveyed the space. "Like I said, it's not done yet. Brian Michaels has been here every day, fixing up one thing or another."

"Oh, my." Violet turned around, her hand over her heart. "I knew what it looked like on paper, and when we went through it those other times, I could see where you were going with it, but this… it doesn't even look like a house."

"Is that a good thing?"

"I suppose so. It's not going to be a regular house anymore, is it? I have the annex, and you'll be upstairs, but it's a business now." Violet set her purse on the table. "Show me around."

Penny kept an eye on her aunt, hoping the changes hadn't upset her. "You'll love the workroom, and you're welcome to use it if you need more space."

"I think I'll be fine. I'll have so much more room to spread out my things here."

Aunt Violet's things had been spread out through the basement of Penny's parents' house for years, in totes labeled with spidery writing that Penny didn't even try to decipher.

"Well, did you decide where you want tables and chairs?"

"Oh, yes. Brian is getting everything set up, just the way I want it." She tapped her cane on the floor as she explored the foyer, inspecting the closet and peering out the front window. "I talked to him yesterday about storage. I know just how I want it arranged, and he says he has a plan."

"I'm sure he does," Penny said. "He's really good, but he likes to make his own plans. Yesterday, he replaced all the soft white light bulbs I'd just put in the consultation area. I like the white LED bulbs in the work areas, but the brides need softer light. He doesn't get that."

"He's an engineer," Violet said. "He was telling me all about the things he'd do differently if he was starting from scratch. He was mostly interested in the lighting and electricity, of course. Outlets and things like that, especially in the big workroom. Seemed to think it should be different—not that he was criticizing the other electricians, of course."

"Of course not. He doesn't criticize. He just redoes it." Penny rolled her eyes. "He did come up with some good ideas. He set up a pressing station with an overhead outlet and hook to keep the cord out of the way. I think it'll be especially useful for your quilting, because you won't have to drag the cord over the fabric."

She led the way into the consultation area, tapped the light switch and groaned as a ghastly brilliance flooded the room. "See? I told him I need good natural light, but I'm not landing airplanes or performing surgery. I'll have to change these back before we open. Later, so he doesn't find out."

Her aunt chuckled. "You don't want to hurt his feelings, or are you afraid he'll change them back again?"

Penny smiled in response. "Maybe both. Like you said, he's an engineer. He thinks he knows the best way to do everything and wants to help me by doing it. He finds this an interesting challenge. I'm not going to stop him. I like the new pressing station. He also put one of my dummies on a turntable. I saw that on Pinterest and printed out a picture of it. He just saw it pinned to my bulletin board and made it for me."

Violet moved through the open spaces, stopping to touch things and look out windows. Penny waited, hoping it wasn't painful for her aunt to see her childhood home broken up.

"Your office was my father's bedroom," Violet said. "The rest were upstairs."

"I wish I'd seen it as it was back then."

When Violet disappeared into the kitchen, Penny followed her. Her aunt stood at the sink, gazing out the window. She spoke without turning around.

"I can't tell you how many hours I spent right here on this spot. It wasn't a very happy place, when I was a girl, but then nieces and nephews came along. They'd run back and forth out there, laughing and playing games I never understood. And then great-nieces and nephews, and now there are great-grand-nieces and nephews. The farm is gone, but the family continues. That's what matters."

"Are you okay with all the changes?" asked Penny. "I don't want to change things that are important to you." It was too late, of course. She'd already made all the changes.

Violet gave Penny a quick hug. "The people are important. There was nothing special to me in this building. I'd rather see you fix it up into something useful than see it crumble away empty."

"I hope you'll be comfortable in the annex," Penny began.

"Stop. You've said that a hundred times," Violet said. "It's a big place, and you've fixed it up beautifully. I don't even have to enter the main house to get to my living quarters. I'll have more privacy than I've had in... forever."

"But you'll have to go outside and walk around the house whenever you want to come over here. I'll keep it shoveled, but still... we should have made a connecting interior door. We still could."

"Not necessary." Violet pointed at the open staircase. "I haven't seen your living quarters, though."

"It's nowhere near ready. It'll be done enough that we can move in at the beginning of the year, but I want to finish up the downstairs first." They mounted the stairs slowly, Penny relaxing as Violet's approval and enthusiasm increased.

"I have a little kitchenette here, and I can use the full kitchen downstairs if I need to." She pointed to a gabled end that had once been the master bedroom. "Dining room and living room are in there, and on the other end, I have my own bedroom and an office I can use as a guest room. A big bathroom, too."

"A whole apartment." Violet patted her arm. "You've done a wonderful job on this place, and it sounds like you've done it on a shoestring."

"I had a lot of volunteer help, so the biggest expenses were plumbers and electricians, the paving of the driveway, permits, and things like that. Dad managed all of that, but now I have to learn the business end of things. Sewing made a good income for me while I was living at home with no expenses, but if I'm going to make a real business of it, and support myself, I have to learn about accounting and marketing and legal things."

"Legal things?" Her aunt laughed. "I suppose you'd better. I'd hate to see you get arrested for unlawful embroidery."

"I think it's more about taxes and licenses. I'm going to need your help with all the forms I have to fill out."

"My pleasure." Violet led the way down the stairs. "Just let me know when you need something."

"I got an email from the Chamber of Commerce. They'll gladly take my money and grant me entrance to their club."

"What about the mentorship program?"

"They said someone would be contacting me." Penny shrugged. "I'm sure it'll be helpful, but I should have waited until I was all settled in here."

"Well, it seems to me that you want to put your best foot forward. Start as you mean to go on."

"A stitch in time saves nine, and make hay while the sun shines," Penny said. "Why are there so many clichés about that kind of thing?"

They laughed as they left the house—the shop— but came to a stop at the sight of a tall man emerging from a gray Subaru.

He straightened and waved. "Hi there!" He loped forward, long dark curls bobbing around his head, and reached out to shake Violet's hand. "You must be Penelope Anderson, the seamstress. I'm Liam Ferra, from the Entrepreneur Mentorship Program." He turned to Penny with an expectant smile.

Penny blinked. Dimples, brown eyes, white teeth, and a cleft chin. Maybe the hair wasn't really too long. It seemed to fit.

She shook his hand. "Hello, Liam. I'm Penelope Anderson. This is my aunt, Violet Anderson."

Liam smote his forehead. "That will teach me to jump to conclusions based on an old-fashioned name and a skilled profession rarely seen in this modern age. I apologize to both of you." He bowed.

What a charming man. So few people realized that dressmaking was a highly-skilled, creative profession. Penny beamed at him.

"I wasn't expecting you so soon. Welcome! I was just showing my aunt what her childhood home looks like now."

"It's quite a change," Violet said. "Very impressive."

"This is your shop? Can I see it?" He looked from Penny to Violet. "Or were you just leaving?"

"Go ahead and give him the tour, Penny. I'll wait out here." Violet waved her cane toward the car. "It's a beautiful day."

"I don't want to inconvenience you," Liam said. "Let's make an appointment."

He meant it, Penny realized. He wasn't hoping to be dissuaded.

"Okay. How about tomorrow? In the morning. Early. Eight?" No one could say Penelope Anderson was slow to grasp an opportunity.

"I'm going to be gone for the weekend." Liam pulled out his phone and tapped on the screen. "Let me check with the boss and see if he needs me on Monday."

"You have a boss? I thought you mentored people who want to be entrepreneurs."

He looked up and gave her a smile. White teeth, dimples, and all. "That's what I went to school for, but a business consultant entrepreneur needs to get a start with an established company first, building a portfolio and reputation."

"Just as I need to do." Penny watched him type out his text. He sounded confident, but a college education and warm brown eyes weren't enough to make him the best adviser for her business. "Reputation and a good portfolio. I have done my research, you know. I even took some business classes at college."

Her aunt broke in before Liam could respond. "You promised to take Sarah to the cities on Monday."

"I can't do Monday, either," Liam said. "What about Tuesday, in the afternoon?"

"That should be fine." Penny was already regretting her rudeness. "Two o'clock here? Do I need to have anything prepared?"

"If you email me a copy of your business plan, I could take a look at it ahead of time. Then we'll just go through a list of questions and get to know each other." He gave her a business card and another smile. "Nothing intimidating."

"Can you email me a list of the questions?"

"I can do that." He slid his phone back into his pocket. "I'll send it as soon as I get back to the office. But

33

it's not a quiz—just questions about your business and goals."

"I like to be prepared. I'll email you the business plan." She waved his card in farewell. "See you Tuesday."

4

This is the real reason I came home." Brian looked at his plate with satisfaction. "Your mom's chicken and potato hotdish. And the desserts. They always have more desserts than regular food at Riverdale potlucks."

"Don't talk to me about chickens," Penny said. "Yesterday was butchering day. I think I'll just have some salad."

"You couldn't get out of that, huh?" Brian chuckled. "You used to come up with excuses and be busy every year. I remember one year you used a red pen to draw measles on yourself."

Penny wrinkled her nose. "Yeah, that one didn't work."

"And another year, you offered to clean the church. For free."

"That one backfired. Mom told the pastor I wasn't available on Saturday, but I'd be happy to do it every Friday for the next month."

"She did try to get out of it." Aunt Violet spooned corn onto her plate. "She tried to make a date with her new business adviser."

Brian stopped, his hand hovering over the plate of dinner rolls. "Oh, yeah?"

"It wasn't a date." Penny nudged him. "You're

holding up the line. We were trying to schedule an appointment. A business appointment."

"Hm." Brian balanced a roll on top of his overloaded plate. "Good-looking guy?"

"Only if you like them tall, dark, and handsome," Violet said.

"Just a business meeting." Penny grabbed a brownie and stalked away from the buffet line.

Violet followed. "I shouldn't have teased you about that young man."

"It's just business," Penny insisted, "but it's embarrassing. There are two seats over there by Mom and Dad. Let's get them before Brian does."

"He's a nice boy." Violet set her plate on the table and lowered herself into the chair Penny's dad pulled out for her. "Thank you, Carl."

"Who's a nice boy?"

"She was talking about Brian. He was giving me a hard time about making excuses for missing chicken day."

"I appreciate you being there," her mother said. "Every year, I have fewer helpers. Pretty soon I'll have to give up the meat chickens altogether."

"There are fewer of us to feed, though. I'll be in my own home this time next year." Penny took a bite of her brownie. "Of course, I've never been much of a cook. I might still show up at suppertime."

"You'll come back for Sunday dinner," her father said, "and we always have chicken for that."

"Sure. And if you need me, I'll be there to butcher chickens. It's only once a year."

"We'll see. Chicken's awfully cheap at the grocery store." Constance sipped her coffee, grimaced and set the Styrofoam cup on the table. "Everything else is delicious. I don't know why they can't make decent coffee."

"You need to put eggs in it," Violet said. "That makes the best coffee. Kristina used to make gallons of it every day for Papa and the boys."

"The boys were what… sixty?" Carl asked.

"As far back as I can remember. We used a big enamel pot, and we'd keep it on the wood stove in the winter, so there was always hot coffee."

Penny leaned forward. "Was the whole house heated with a wood stove?"

"I think it was when I was a little girl," Violet said, "but we had coal and then oil later. There wasn't any heat upstairs."

"We had propane and central heat by the time I moved out."

Violet continued as if Carl hadn't spoken. "Papa built a bedroom for himself downstairs. He said it was because the boys snored, and it was too cold upstairs, but I think he just liked being alone. He could stay up late or go to bed early and no one would notice or care."

"He never remarried," Constance said.

"Who would have him?" Violet pushed her plate away. "Eight children and a farm to run? He might have liked the company of a wife, but it would have been difficult, with Kristina. She'd been running the house since she was sixteen years old."

"She didn't want to get married and move to a home of her own?" Now that the house was hers, the family history intrigued Penny. If Violet had ever discussed it before, she hadn't listened.

"I don't think so. Kristina did what she wanted to, so if she'd wanted to get married, she'd have done it—whether the groom wanted it or not."

"Are you sure you want to do this today?" Violet pulled her bag from the back seat. Apparently, it was a moot question. "This is a busy time for you."

"No, this is a good time. But like I said, I've never done a quilt before." Or wanted to. She made bridal gowns, not patchwork quilts. Quilts were for old ladies and babies.

"If you can sew dresses, you can sew a quilt. It's all straight lines, and it's flat."

"If you say so." Penny noticed her aunt's expression and gave herself a mental shake. She owed Violet a lot more than a few hours of her time. "Brian got the cutting mat set up on the big worktable, and my good shears are newly sharpened."

"We won't need your shears for this one. It's all rotary cut."

"The whole thing?" Penny perked up. She could use a rotary cutter.

"The whole thing. I brought my own rulers." Violet pointed. "They're all in that Rubbermaid tote. I wasn't sure what you had."

"So, what do we need to do first?"

Violet led the way back to the workroom. "All the

fabric's washed and pressed and ready to cut."

"Okay!" Maybe it wouldn't take too long. "What do you want me to do?"

"You can keep me company. Thread the sewing machine needle."

Taken aback, Penny dropped the tote next to the table. "That's all? I thought you needed help."

"I do," Violet said. "I need your company. And I guess you can probably do some of the cutting and sewing."

"I can do that!" Penny eyed her with concern. "Why don't you sit down and tell me about the pattern."

Her aunt sank onto the small blue chair and fidgeted with the handle of her bag. Penny waited.

"Last time I made a quilt, I cut some of the pieces too big."

"That's better than cutting them too small, isn't it?"

Violet didn't meet her eyes. "I didn't notice it at first, and I sewed a lot of it together before I realized the quilt didn't come together right. I was mad and in a hurry, so I wasn't as careful as I should have been, and I sewed through my thumbnail." She held up her left hand and Penny winced.

"Ouch. I've done that a couple times."

"But I'm on blood thinners, you know, and it made a mess." She gave an unconvincing chuckle. "Fortunately, no one was around to see it. But then I started worrying about using the rotary cutter. When I stand up too long, my hands get a little shaky. That's why I like my family quilts better. I can do them by hand while I watch television."

Relieved that they weren't making one of the ugly crazy quilts, Penny opened the tote and withdrew acrylic rulers and other tools. "So, what are we making?"

"I'm calling this one the Christmas Glory Quilt. It's going to be a Christmas present for your aunt Colleen. I'd hoped to get down there for Christmas, but I'm not going to make it this year. Maybe in February or March, when I'm ready for a warmer climate."

"That would be the time to visit Florida," Penny said. "Besides, we want you here with us for Christmas, especially since Grandma's down there."

"It will be fun, with all of you. Especially Sadie. She's the perfect Christmas age."

"Eight is a good age," Penny agreed. She launched into talk of the quilt. "So, if it's all straight lines, how hard can it be?"

Violet opened her mouth and Penny held up a hand, laughing. "No, don't tell me. I was joking. Just tell me what to do. But you may have to hold my hand while I learn."

"The first part is the hardest. All the pieces have to be cut perfectly. You use the lines on the ruler and the mat together to measure."

Penny's good humor fled. "You know I can't do that." She picked up one of the rulers. "This has so many numbers and lines close together. I'd make a mess of it."

"No, no," her aunt interrupted. "I had an idea. I'm going to mark the ruler with tape, and you just have to line up the tape with the lines on the mat and the edge of the fabric."

Penny rubbed her eyes as if in anticipation of the

headache such work would bring on. "I'd make a mess of it," she repeated.

"Can we try? If the tape doesn't work, some people have used sticky notes. And I've seen you use tape to measure seam allowances. I think it would work."

"Well, let's start with a couple scrap pieces before we cut into your good fabric." Penny nodded at the stack of green and white fabrics Violet was unloading from her bag. "I don't want to ruin that. Or—what if I got you a stool? You could sit down and cut, and I could do the sewing."

"Just try it."

Her aunt's soothing tone didn't ease Penny's fears. It was one thing to cut satin or chiffon along the edge of a pattern or on a triple-measured line. Cutting was easy, but this kind of measuring would keep her tense.

"I brought some fabric we can use for prototypes."

"Prototypes?" Penny asked. "That's intimidating."

"Just a trial block. I've drafted out the pattern, but I haven't actually made it yet. There are usually some changes to make once you start working." Violet handed Penny a stack of paper.

"It looks like a dress pattern, all line drawings."

"Yes," her aunt nodded. "But it has to be cut right first." She took the papers from Penny's hands and pulled out one of them. "This is the cutting chart. We check off the pieces as we cut them. Don't worry," she added hastily. "I'll be right there."

An hour later, in spite of the cool October evening, Penny was sweating and, as she had anticipated, her head ached.

"Are you warm? I could turn the air conditioning on."

Violet didn't look up. "Forty-three, forty-four, forty-five. No, dear, I'm comfortable."

Penny walked over to open a window. "I suppose you didn't have air-conditioning when you lived here."

"Oh, no. It was hot, and even hotter when we were younger and there was so much work to do in the kitchen. We were still cooking and canning a lot back then." She made a check mark on the chart. "All done with the squares."

Penny stalled. "You were the youngest, right? And Kristina was the oldest. I know she and Grandpa died about the same time. And Olof is the only one still living, right?"

"And me, of course. I was the baby of the family." Violet looked around. "It's like a totally different place. It was such a higgledy piggledy house by the time it was done."

"Dad said they kept adding bedrooms because no one ever left."

"That sounds about right. It was fine when it was just the nine of us, and then Dad built himself that bedroom downstairs, so we weren't too crowded. But then Hans and then Karl left, and there was too much space."

"Were they the ones who died in World War Two?"

Violet nodded. "Your father is named after Karl. The house was a sad place after that, until your grandpa married my best friend and she came to live with us. Your

Uncle Scott was born a couple years later, and my brother Alex got married and his wife came to live with us. After that, there were new babies in the house almost every year."

"All in this house? I didn't know that!"

"That's why it's so big. Papa added his room, and then two more bedrooms when the boys got married, so they had rooms of their own, downstairs." Violet pointed toward the fitting room. "Over there. Then they built the annex, when your grandma was pregnant with your Uncle Gary. Later, they moved into town and Alex and Molly moved into the annex. At one time, we had fifteen people living here."

"Wow! You really did do a lot of cooking, but at least you had other women to help."

"Yes, but I went to work for the post office, you know, so I wasn't home during the day. Molly was a teacher, so only your grandma was here with Kristina. And then she moved into the annex and was busy with her children and Molly's, too, so Kristina did most of the cooking and housework." Violet shrugged. "She liked it that way."

"She liked to do all the work?"

"Kristina didn't like people messing with her arrangements. She liked it when people admired her for taking care of Papa and the boys." Violet rubbed her forehead. "Being here brings back memories. I was born here and lived here for 66 years, and now I'm back. I think we can stop now. It's getting late."

5

At 1:59, the gray Subaru swept into the driveway. Penny watched Liam climb out, retrieve a leather case from the back seat, and click the key fob to lock the doors. City boy. He wore slim-fitting tan slacks with a loose indigo blue shirt. Business casual for central Minnesota. She'd be underdressed in her jeans and pink hoodie. Good.

Penny waited until he knocked before opening the door. His wide smile was just as bright as she'd remembered it, and it took a minute for her to remember why he was there.

"Hi. Come on in."

"Hello." He stepped inside. "Should I take my shoes off?"

"No, Dad says that's a business liability. I might get sued if someone steps on a pin or stubs their toe."

"Zoning and insurance rule the world," Liam said. "Business 101. This is a big farmhouse. If you were closer to the lake, it would be a good bed and breakfast."

"Well, maybe six months ago, but there aren't any bedrooms left."

Liam raised dark, expressive eyebrows. "What happened to them?" He followed her around the corner and stopped. "This is nice!"

"Thank you!" Penny flushed with pleasure at his

compliment. "I'm really pleased with it. As you can see, I opened up all the rooms, so they connect, but they're still separate places. To the left is the consultation space. That's a big room because we do most of the design work in there. Then there's an area for showing off the dresses—trying them on—a large fitting room, and a changing room. That room has a door, for privacy. Then we loop back around to the workroom."

Liam turned in a circle, interest lighting his face. "It looks comfortable everywhere, with all the tables and chairs, not like a retail store. You're selling people an experience, not just a dress."

"Right!" His insight was unexpected. Penny spread her arms. "It's not just about having a pretty dress. Women who come here get to design their gown and be involved with its creation. They select fabrics and accessories. Actually," she amended, "I design the dress with their input and have them come for several fittings."

"I see." Liam nodded several times. "That's how you can attract clients from the cities. It's not just buying a dress or even having one made. You're going to be expensive and worth every penny. Um... that was unintended."

"My dad and brothers are always making penny jokes. Anyhow, that's what I'm thinking. But... I don't want to only work with rich people. In fact..." Penny looked at her feet. Liam was here to help her grow a profitable business, so she should be honest with him. "I also want to do it as a ministry."

He looked confused. "A ministry?"

"Yes. Not all the time. I want to set up Penny

Anderson Designs as an upscale bridal shop. An experience. But sometimes, I'm going to do the same thing for women who can't afford my usual prices. The whole thing, start to finish. And, well, I'm not comfortable with pricing that excludes my friends."

He held up a hand. "We'll talk about that, but first show me the rest of the house."

Had he understood what she was saying? Her qualms resurfaced. She didn't want to be a high-powered businesswoman.

"Okay, but it's important to me."

He nodded. "We'll talk about it. I want to see the rest of the house!"

"All right." Penny ushered him through the consultation area. "There's a full kitchen over there, and this is my office." She opened the mullion door and waited for him to enter ahead of her. "I won't be using this room much, but I wanted a private place for the mess."

"Good idea." He walked over to the window.

Penny followed him into the small room. "My aunt will be helping me with accounting and paperwork. Should we get her involved in our mentoring sessions?"

Liam's curls swayed as he shook his head. "No, because entrepreneurship isn't about the bookkeeping. Entrepreneurship is a business mindset. Your business will thrive or fail according to you."

"Well, I am aware of that, since I am the one doing all the work. Except for the accounting, of course. But, yeah... it's all on me. I do all of it. That's what being self-employed means, right?" She regretted the sarcasm as soon as it left her mouth. What was the matter with her lately?

"No, not really. Do you have to do all of it? Is there any reason you can't hire someone and be more productive? Wait, no. We can talk about that later, too. Show me the rest of it."

"There's not much else to see. Those stairs go up to my living quarters, and the whole south wing of the house is Aunt Violet's, but we won't be moving in until the beginning of the year."

She closed the door behind them. "I may hire an employee to clean and wash windows. All these little panes are a pain."

Liam chuckled. "Hiring a cleaning person is a good idea. A sole proprietor can get burned out if he or she tries to do everything, especially the boring parts like cleaning. If you hire someone from an agency, you won't have employer expenses."

"Ha. I'll hire someone from the Anderson agency. I have several siblings who'd jump at the chance to earn some cash."

"Several!" Liam turned to look at her. "How many are there?"

"Three brothers and three sisters. But I admit, only the youngest three would be willing, and Jeffrey might try to negotiate himself out of my budget."

"I'm an only child."

"Really." Penelope regarded him with interest. "Aside from little kids, I only know one other only child, and she's unbearably perfect."

"Yeah, that goes with the territory. Unbearable

perfection." He grinned. "Are you ready to get started?" He lifted the briefcase he still carried. "Let's sit down."

"Great." Penny perched on the edge of the chair. He said they would just get to know each other in this first session. She'd had the computer read his questions to her, and if he stuck to that script, she was prepared. If he wanted her to read things, she was in trouble.

Liam started rummaging in his case as he sat on the brown leather couch. "I went through your business plan. It looks pretty standard."

It should; she'd used a template from one of the few business courses she'd taken in college.

"Clean and simple," Liam continued. "That's the best kind. It gives you flexibility. Paring back the analysis gives you a realistic range for your goals and projections."

He probably knew what he was talking about, but the dimples—and the curls—made it hard to take him seriously. Was he Spanish? Greek?

"Where did you get that data?"

Penny jumped, hoping she hadn't been mooning like a lovesick puppy. "I'm sorry. What data?"

"Your demographics. Now that I have a better idea of your vision for this place, I think you should revisit that. It sounds like you're on point for St. Cloud and Duluth, with all the colleges, but I think you can reach a more upscale market in the cities."

"Okay," Penny said, "but I don't want to price myself out of the local market."

"That's fine. A really exclusive retailer doesn't put price tags on the merchandise. You can price your dresses according to the customer. You can even give them away if you want. That's the freedom that comes in being an entrepreneur."

"Speaking of being an entrepreneur," Penny said, "I did some research after I signed up for your program, and it seems to me that I'm just self-employed, not an entrepreneur. I provide the service to the customer, and without me, there's no business. An entrepreneur establishes companies that become self-sustaining. Right?"

Liam rubbed his nose. "The terms overlap, but you're right. Your growth is limited by your own ability to produce." He smiled at her. "Your business—as it is now—isn't scalable. You can't grow indefinitely by increasing your sales volume."

Penny frowned. "What do you mean?"

"Let's say you can make two wedding dresses a month, including all of your consultations, fittings, sewing, shopping and whatever else you need to do to make a dress. No marketing or business management—just making and selling a dress." He leaned forward, elbows on his knees, hands clasped. "You can make two a month."

"Actually, I could probably do three, if they're timed right."

"Okay, three. So, what happens when a fourth bride comes in? Are you able to make her a dress? What if five or six clients show up in a month?"

"I don't know. I'm still not getting a consistent three."

"But you will," Liam said. "My point is, you only have a certain amount of time. So, your time is like money, and you have to budget it like it's money."

"It's not scalable," Penny repeated. "I can't just take on more clients to make more money. So, if I want to increase my profit, I have to decrease my expenses or increase my prices."

He nodded. "Right. That's basic business principles."

"So, I'm not an entrepreneur."

"The mentoring program really focuses on small businesses and self-employed people who want to grow," Liam admitted, "but if you are starting a small business, learning as much as you can and investing money in it, you're an entrepreneur." He warmed to the topic. "It's a state of mind. An entrepreneur thinks about building a business that succeeds long-term. He—she—has a vision of something and works toward that vision, knowing that success is behind it. Look at this place. You had a vision."

"And now I need a plan. The more I learn, the more overwhelmed I feel."

"I hope I can help with that!" He stood. "We didn't get to that list of questions. We ran out of time. Are Tuesday afternoons good for you?"

"That's fine. I'm not even really open yet."

"You're going to be a success, Penny." His gaze was warm. Affirming. Was that part of the program?

"I'm going to try." She waved goodbye as he pointed the key fob at the SUV and strolled down the walkway. This mentorship thing was going to be more interesting than she'd expected.

6

I 'll be praying for you. Let me know if I can do anything to help."

Penny paused in the doorway, not wanting to interrupt Brian's call, but he saw her and beckoned. Bossy.

After a few seconds, he continued, "That's generous of you. I'll see you on November fourth. Get well!" He slid the phone into his pocket and greeted her with a smile. "Morning, sunshine. I didn't expect to see you here so early."

"I didn't expect to see you, either. What are you painting?"

He lifted the can. "The bathroom. I made a mess when I added an outlet behind the vanity, so I need to touch up that wall. Turns out I won't be starting work for a few weeks yet. The owner of the company is having surgery, and he can't trust anyone else to train me. Sounds like he's got control issues."

Penny snorted. It wasn't ladylike, but Brian just grinned. He picked up a paintbrush and plastic sheeting and headed toward the bathroom, whistling. He'd always been able to whistle songs, but she could do a better come-home-now whistle. Not that it was a competition, of course.

She followed him. "Have you seen my aunt? I

thought she was going to be here today."

"She was out back when I got here." Brian pried the paint can open.

"Outside? It's only fifty degrees out there!"

He looked up. "She's an adult. She'll come in if she's cold."

Penny ignored that. "I'd better go check on her."

She found Violet in the far corner of the back yard. The older woman looked up when she called out and waited for Penny to reach her.

"I was looking for some hostas that used to be back here." She pointed. "Maria and I put that rock path in there, and we planted perennials, but they don't appear to have survived."

"Maybe they've died off for the year," Penny said. "It's been getting pretty cold at night."

"Maybe." Violet prodded a pile of sodden leaves with her cane. "It really was a pretty garden."

"I remember it. I thought it looked like a fairyland. There were gnomes, weren't there? And those little Dutch children. The boy and the girl bending forward to kiss each other."

"You remember that? You were just a little girl then." Violet poked at more leaves. "I gave those to your cousin Marlys when we moved out."

"We could put some flowers back here," Penny said.

"But not the gnomes and kissing children." Violet chuckled. "They wouldn't go with your country chic theme."

"The back yard doesn't have to be country chic. I

was thinking of putting a patio back here. We could put up a table and chairs and maybe one of those portable fire pits. You said you used to sit out here."

"When it had a view of the river." Her aunt looked at the trees as if she could see through them, remembering a different vista. "That would be nice."

Penny tapped on the light switch and enjoyed a rush of pleasure and excitement at the sight of her new studio. After years of working in her parents' spare bedroom, this spacious workshop inspired her to design and create.

Humming along with the radio, she examined each piece of gleaming fabric before setting it in the sewing machine. No blood stains. The work went smoothly, and an hour later, she slid the bodice over the dressmaker's dummy. A perfect fit. She beamed at it.

"Nice."

She turned at the sound of Brian's voice. "It turned out well. The ironing station is genius."

"Is that the fabric I bled all over after you broke my nose?"

"You can't even tell." Penny hid a smile. He shouldn't have been hiding behind the door.

"Want some lunch?"

"Lunch! Is it that late? I have an appointment at two."

"There's plenty of time." His charming smile made her blink. Brian had grown into a good-looking man, especially when he smiled like that.

She glanced at the heap of blue chiffon on the cutting table. She really should work on the flower girl dresses instead of going off to lunch. If she got hungry, she could microwave a boxed meal from the freezer.

"Oh, come on. My treat."

"Your treat?" Penny grabbed a sheet and tossed it over the dummy. "How could I resist that?"

Penny leaned back against the seat and admired the wooden cross hanging from the rear-view mirror. It didn't even swing when Brian shifted gears. He drove his truck better than she did. The pickup was a good fit for him—not new or expensive, but clean and reliable.

"You're smiling." Brian looked over and caught her gaze. "What are you thinking about?"

She probably shouldn't share her thoughts. "You."

"Me? I'm glad I make you smile."

"I'm glad you came back to Milaca. I missed you!"

"Thanks. I missed you, too."

She chuckled. "You did not. I'm pretty sure you were too busy at college and work to think about me. So, what are you doing while you wait to start your new job—other than work on my shop?"

"I'm building myself a house." He meant to sound nonchalant, but she could hear the pride in his voice.

"A house! Building it yourself, you mean, or having a contractor build it?"

"What do you think?"

She laughed. "Never mind. Are you doing everything?"

"I got someone to dig and pour the foundation," he

admitted. "It's a log home, with a walkout basement. Not big, but big enough."

"That's great! Where is it?"

"About halfway between here and Princeton, a mile and a half off 169. We could go there after lunch, if you like."

"I can't. I have an appointment with my 'mentor.'" She put the word in air quotes.

"Meeting with Mr. Tall-dark-and-handsome?"

"It's a business meeting. I think it's going to be helpful, even though he doesn't quite understand how I can operate as a ministry and a profitable business—or why I want to."

"He doesn't know you," Brian replied.

Penny twisted in her seat to look at him. "But what if I'm doing it wrong? Statistically, most businesses fail within the first few years. I was annoyed with Dad when he said I had to sign up for this, but I'm glad I did. I thought I knew what I was doing, but now I'm worried. Liam says the problem with my business is that it's not scalable. I can't increase my income by making more sales. I do the designing and the sewing and the sales—meeting with clients—and the shopping, marketing and a dozen other things. My income isn't going to increase over time, except that my prices might go up, and that's usually because the costs of materials go up. I'm already frugal with materials and overhead expenses." She took a deep breath. "Sorry. I didn't mean to dump all that on you."

Brian reached over and tapped her knee. "Hey. You've got a problem."

Penny stopped and scowled. "Is that supposed to be reassuring?"

"Were you looking for reassurance?" His tone was cautious.

"No, not really. But you're always jumping in with good ideas."

"Oh, no." He shook his head emphatically. "That's one thing my mother taught me. When a woman is telling you her problems, she doesn't want you to fix things."

"What? You're always fixing things for me!"

"That's different."

"So, when I have a real problem, you aren't going to help?" She asked with incredulity.

"Um… did you want help?"

"Brian!"

"Mom says that a woman wants her husband to hear her and acknowledge that her concerns are valid." He said it like a quotation. "Is that wrong?"

"But…" She fell silent, unable to formulate an appropriate response.

His face reddened. "I'm not your husband, but we're friends. It seemed like a good time to take Mom's advice."

Brian would make a very good husband. Mrs. Michaels had her issues, but she'd raised great kids.

"She's right. You just took me by surprise. It is nice to have someone listen and not just rush in with reassurance."

"But do you need to make more money?" He cast a sidelong glance at her and slowed as they entered the city limits.

"Probably, if I need to support myself long-term. I'd like to have some savings. Being self-employed is expensive, especially for insurance. And taxes." She grimaced.

Brian drove in silence and then spoke as if choosing his words. "Don't take this the wrong way, but you probably won't need to support yourself forever. You'll get married, and whether you keep working or not, your husband will make an income, too."

"I don't know." Penny looked out the window at a row of retired farmers sitting in rockers on the porch of The Koffee Kupp. They looked comfortable. "Maybe I'll just be an aunt."

He scoffed. "You'll get married. I'm surprised you're not married already. Are all the local guys blind and stupid?"

She rolled her eyes but was unable to suppress a smile. Brian did have his own style of charm. "It's not quite that simple. Why aren't you married?"

"Oh, I will someday. I have to finish my house first."

An unexpected anger sparked in Penny. "Oh, that's right. You have to have a house before you get married."

Brian parked the truck on the gravel lot and frowned at her. "What are you talking about?"

"That's what your mom said, remember? She quoted the Bible verse about building the house and planting the fields before you take a wife and have a family. You were there. She was talking about Jim, and the fact that he and Faith would have to rent an apartment."

He rubbed the back of his neck. "I do remember that, but there was more to the story. She loves Jim now. It was a hard time for her. She'd always had this perfect family fantasy. She thought we would grow up and marry people from our own church and raise our children there, and we'd all be one happy extended family. If she just followed a certain set of rules, everything would be perfect and safe."

Didn't he see it? His mother was the most legalistic Christian Penny had ever met. His father was almost as bad.

"The thing is," Brian said as he opened the door, "Mom may be judgmental, but she's not a hypocrite. She lives out her convictions. But she has this idea that it's her responsibility to raise up her children to be perfect Christians, and she's afraid of failing. When Faith came home and announced she was marrying a man they'd never met, Mom was upset."

Penny had been upset, too, but young enough to be thrilled by her friend's love-at-first-sight romance. She hopped out of the truck and met Brian at the door. He looked down at her, clearly wanting to express something. She waited.

"Mom doesn't have real trust in God. She thinks she does, but she worries about everything—especially us kids. She believes in God, in Jesus and His work of salvation, but she feels like He has high expectations for her and she's determined to do all the right things—not for her salvation, but out of obedience." He hesitated. "Do you understand what I mean? She thinks she's responsible for our spiritual condition. She doesn't just think Faith is wrong for going to a different church, using a different version of the Bible and sending Angel to the public school. She's afraid for them. I wish she could understand that God won't judge her for our failures— and that He'll love us even if we aren't following the rules she believes in." He shrugged. "She just wants us to be all right."

7

P enny? Where are you?" Liam's enthusiastic calls resounded from the walls and wood floors.

"Hey, Liam." Her mentor's natural friendliness had quickly replaced his initial formality, but he wasn't usually this ebullient. Penny hastened out to greet him. "What's going on?"

"I have a client for you! A good one!"

"Oh. Thank you!" She wondered if she should pat him on the head, like a golden retriever who'd fetched an especially juicy tennis ball. "Is she a friend of yours?"

"She's my boss's niece. Her name's Danielle Lorris, and she's the regional director for the Gamma Kamma Pi's, so she knows a lot of the other young SCSU women who might get married soon."

"Gamma Kamma what?"

"It's a sorority, and I guess she's responsible for all the chapters in Minnesota, Wisconsin... the Midwest. It's a pretty big one, nationwide. Dani—she likes to be called Dani—is marrying a lobbyist or political advisor of some kind, so there are hundreds of people on the guest list. It'll be great exposure for you."

"It sounds big." Probably too big for her. It was nice of Liam to think of her, though. "When is the wedding?"

"New Year's Eve. A Minnesota winter wedding."

He sounded like an advertising agent, smug and confident in his grand idea.

"Next year, you mean? Not this year."

"No, this year. That's the point. She bought a dress, and her house burned down, so she needs a new one." He nodded, eyes alight, dimples in full force.

"By New Year's Eve? This New Year's Eve?"

"That's the beauty of it. You'll be able to get it done before you move into your apartment here, so you won't be trying to sew and move at the same time."

Penny opened her mouth and shut it again. He had good intentions, and he was her business mentor!

"I gave her your phone number and address," Liam said, "but I'd be happy to bring her over and introduce you. I think you'll like her."

"But New Year's Eve... it's so soon. I'm nowhere near ready to receive clients here. Usually, I have the initial consultation at the bride's home—but it burned down? —or at my parents', which won't impress her with my professionalism."

"You can have it ready." Liam looked around. "What's left to be done?"

"Some of everything!" She stood, looking at his animated face, and tried to explain. "Liam, a bridal gown takes a long time. If she came right away and her dress isn't too complicated, and if the fabric is readily available, I could probably get it done, but it's such short notice!"

"She seemed pretty worried about that. I told her even though your building is new, you have a lot of experience. I wish you'd got your website updated. Have you found someone to do it yet?

"No. But..." It was useless. She couldn't refuse to take a client Liam brought her. They'd spent an hour yesterday, brainstorming ways to use an online presence to attract new clients.

"Okay, Liam. I'll meet with her, but she may not want me at all. Thank you for thinking of me."

Dani Lorris was a Liamette. The physical resemblance ended at the dimples, bright white smile and big brown eyes. The rest of her was short, curvy, and sweet. Unlike Liam's corkscrew curls that bobbed with his every movement, her shiny brown hair was cut in a poufy bob that stacked in the back and swung longer in front. But like Liam, Dani radiated enthusiasm and displayed a friendly interest in Penny's personal life as well as her business.

"I'm so glad I came! This place is darling. Liam says you're the best bridal gown designer in the state."

"He did?" Penny paused in the act of hanging up Dani's coat. "I'm not sure he's really qualified to make that assessment."

Dani laughed. Musically, of course. "It did make me wonder if the two of you are... together?"

"Oh, no," Penny said. "He's my business mentor. I think he finds me a challenge."

"He thinks you can work miracles. I tried to tell him you can't just whip up a wedding gown like a souffle, but he talked until I gave in. So here I am!" She beamed a Liam-like smile at Penny.

"You're my first client in the new building. Come on in." She fought back the urge to chatter. She always talked too much when she was nervous, and she wanted this consultation to be perfect. "Can I get you some water?"

"No, thanks." Dani sat on the sofa. "I have to tell you; my mother had a meltdown when I told her I was going to come here. She doesn't think a Milaca dressmaker can make the kind of gown I need."

A meltdown. How could she have forgotten? "Liam told me about the fire. I'm sorry."

"Well, it's okay. I didn't really like it, anyways."

Penny blinked, but before she could say anything, Dani continued.

"My sister picked it out, and my mom loved it, but it never felt right to me. My future mother-in-law, the professional educator, said it was too glamorous." She leaned forward and spoke in a conspiratorial whisper. "That might just be why I bought it."

"Do you have a picture of it?"

"I do!" Dani reached for her phone and realized she didn't have it. "Can you hand me my purse?"

Penny handed it to her. "I'm sorry about your house, though."

Dani stopped rummaging in her purse and looked up. "Oh, it wasn't our house. It was the sorority house. I brought it over there to show my friends. I should've just shown them a picture. But silver linings and all that. I must have left my phone in my coat pocket."

She jumped to her feet and headed for the entryway, speaking over her shoulder. "We bought the dress in Chicago, back in May. The four of us made a weekend of it, shopping and taking in a couple shows. I tried on forty dresses. I counted."

Dani returned, tapping on the phone. "Then I went back two more times for fittings. I'm not starting over again. Mom's making calls to places in Minneapolis, but I'm just about ready to buy one on eBay. There. Scroll down to see both pictures.

Penny took the phone and looked at the pictures. Ugh. Had the sorority house been insured? Maybe the fire department should open an arson investigation.

"It looks like a very elegant dress."

Dani tilted her head with a comical expression. "Do I look elegant to you?"

"Well... we've only just met. I'd expect you to be somewhere between classic and trendy." Penny held up the phone. "What did you like about it?"

"The color was pretty. It was off-white. And the fabric was really soft. But I'm not skinny enough to wear something that just drapes over me like that. The saleswoman kept talking about good undergarments, and she recommended high heels to make it hang better."

"This style looks best on someone tall and slender," Penny agreed. "And even they need to wear high heels and good undergarments."

"That gold beading on the hem and train was heavy, too, so I felt like it was dragging down. But the worst part was that low-cut back." Dani scooted closer and pointed at the picture. "All I could think about was what kind of bra I could wear." She hunched her shoulders. "As you can see, I need to wear a bra."

"Okay." Penny returned the phone. "Tell me about your wedding. Afternoon? Evening? Dancing?"

"It's at the Centennial Theater, on New Year's Eve, so we're having an evening wedding, a late supper and dancing til midnight." The men are in black with white shirts and ties, and the bridesmaids are in champagne." Dani rattled off the details, tapping on her phone. "Here. These are the bridesmaids' dresses. My sister picked those out, too. She's the maid of honor."

Penny glanced at the picture without taking the phone. "So, it's pretty formal."

"Traditional. John and his family are prominent members of the community, with a lot of business leaders and politicians on their guest list. They're paying for half the wedding, so..." Dani shrugged. "It'll be a beautiful wedding. Especially if I can get a dress I like."

Penny flipped open a notebook and wrote the words traditional, formal, evening, and dancing. "Have you chosen your flowers?"

"Months ago. Hold on." Dani tapped on the phone again and held it out. "I used Instagram for a while, but it's easier to look at things on Pinterest. Ivory roses, greenery, a bit of pink and lavender."

"Those are beautiful," Penny said. She added ivory roses to the list and pushed the notepad aside. "I didn't take on many clients for this fall, because I knew I'd be moving over here. So, I do have time, if you can be available for consultations and fittings. I make bridal gowns that fit the bride in every way—not just physically, so the first thing we do is design the dress together."

"Really?" Dani bounced on the seat. "Design it

together?"

Penny nodded. "Sometimes brides come to me with a picture or idea and we start there." She relaxed as she fell into the familiar spiel. "You look through those portfolios and tell me what you like—and don't like. I make some preliminary sketches, and we talk. If we're both comfortable after that initial design session, we sign a contract and move forward."

"Can I take the portfolios home? I have to get back to St. Cloud by six." Dani opened the calendar on her phone and looked at Penny expectantly. "I could bring them back tomorrow or Monday for the design appointment. Or Tuesday. Does that work for you?"

Penny waved goodbye, warmed by Dani's exuberant hug. She liked the girl and hoped she could make her a gown, but in Penny's experience, uncooperative mothers and bridesmaids invariably led to trouble.

8

W hat are you doing?" Laughing, Penny stepped over a pile of rocks and approached Brian. "You've been standing out here for at least five minutes, like a scarecrow or a lawn ornament or something."

"I do look good leaning on a shovel." He stabbed the shovel into the ground and walked to meet her. "I was trying to figure out Violet's garden. She said it was over here in this corner, but she might be confused. I think that plot was sold off with the rest of the land, because it was outside the yard."

"That's what you were thinking about for so long?"

"Mostly. I was trying to figure out where she could put a new garden, but there's no sun except right by the house," Brian said.

"She'd be happy if you'd chop down all the trees," Penny said. "Then she could have her view of the river."

"A view of the river? From here?" Brian turned to peer through the trees.

"It was a long time ago, and we don't actually own those trees, so we probably shouldn't cut them down."

"What do you think? Garden? No garden?"

Penny bit her lip. "Dad's got the front and side yards all planned out. I'll tell her we should wait 'til spring. We could probably find a place for all those bulbs, though."

Brian pointed. "Over there. She's got a shrub to go in there, too."

"Um… isn't that where the dogs are buried?" She took a step backward.

"Violet says the dogs are all buried to the left of that tree."

"Violet thought we had a half-acre garden in the back yard," Penny reminded him. "Don't dig too deep."

"Very funny. I'll have to do it tomorrow or the next day. I'm running over to Princeton this afternoon to fill out some paperwork for my new job."

"That's right! You start on the third." Startled, Penny smiled as brightly as she could manage, fighting back irrational tears. "You'll be glad to be back at a real job, putting that expensive degree to good use. I'm sure your work there will be a lot more interesting than all the odd jobs here." She was chattering. "I'm glad you'll be able to get to work, but I'd have been in trouble if you hadn't been here available to help me. It certainly wouldn't have been ready for my new client."

Disappointment gave way to annoyance when he didn't say anything. The big ox. He'd always done that… let her babble until she ran down.

"You're welcome. I saw your new client. How did it go?"

"She signed a contract!"

She took the two steps forward to give him a quick, gleeful hug, but he moved faster.

"All right!" He lifted her from her feet in a hearty

embrace and spun her around. "You did it!"

He stopped, at her laughing protestations, and let her slide to her feet, but he didn't release her. "I'm so proud of you, Penny."

She felt the rumble of his voice in his chest, against her ear, and she was back to tears. She let him hold her, patting her back until she got herself under control. She was glad he'd been here, glad he was the first to hear the good news. If anyone understood what this moment meant to her, it was Brian Michaels.

She gave a final—hopefully final—sniff and moved away. "Thanks. I'm pretty proud of me, too." Enough emotional whiplash. "Have you had lunch? My treat this time."

"No, this is a celebration for you." Brian collected his tools. "My treat. You can tell me about your new client."

"Well, look at that. Mr. Millennial is waiting for you."

"Liam Millennial. That's a mouthful." Penny unbuckled her seat belt. "Thanks for lunch, Brian. I enjoyed it."

"You're welcome." Brian stepped from the truck and swung the door shut.

Penny had to jump. "You're early!"

"Just a little." Liam nodded at Brian and returned his attention to Penny. "I brought you some books on business and marketing for artists."

"I thought you were supposed to teach her that stuff." Brian lounged against his truck. "She's awfully busy already, running a business and getting her work done, not to mention having business appointments with you. When's she supposed to find time to read books?"

Penny gave Brian a quick, grateful smile before turning away and touching Liam's elbow to steer him toward the house. Brian didn't want her embarrassed, but he needed to let her deal with things now. She was 26, not seven years old and begging for his help with her schoolwork. "So, tell me what we're going to do today."

Liam didn't move. "There's no hurry. I don't need them back."

Great. Now he looked like a kicked puppy instead of a bouncy lab. Penny took the books and walked toward the house. "For artists. I like to think of myself that way."

To her relief, Liam followed. "That's what kind of business you have. You sell one-of-a-kind items. Some artists, like painters or photographers, can sell prints in addition to their originals. A writer or musician can publish their work and sell it over and over. But someone doing pottery or glassblowing or sewing can only make and sell something once."

He continued talking as they sat down. "You're also like a dogwalker."

She cast him a startle glance. "A dogwalker? I can be an artist or a dogwalker?"

"Non-scalable. One pit bull, one hour. You can charge more money, but you can't add more pit bulls than you have hours."

"I could walk corgis, two or three at a time."

"Exactly." He bobbed his head in approval. "But wedding gowns aren't corgis. They're pit bulls."

"Oh," Penny said, "simple dresses or costumes would be corgis. I can do those assembly-line style and turn them out by the dozen in the time it takes me to make a wedding dress. A pit bull." She leaned back and regarded Liam thoughtfully. "Is that what you think I should do?"

"No, not at all. You can charge a lot more money for walking a pit bull than a corgi, and there aren't many people who can do it well."

She nodded. "Anyone can walk a corgi."

"Once you have a reputation as a topnotch bridal gown designer, pit bull owners will be competing for your services and you can charge whatever you like and work as many hours as you want to." He stopped. "That didn't come out right."

Penny's chuckles grew into open laughter. "I get it. All those pit bull brides." She wiped tears from her eyes. "And the poor corgi walker has to keep walking a whole pack of corgis all the time, unable to take a break, and always worried that she can be replaced by a younger, more energetic corgi walker." She snorted. "A corgi walker wannabe."

"The metaphor starts breaking down there," Liam said. "And I'm not sure corgis are a great example if you mean a well-behaved dog who won't give you any trouble."

"And I'm not sure pit bulls should be used in connection with brides. Maybe some mothers, but most of them are friendly. Speaking of which, thank you for sending Dani Lorris to me. I'm making her dress."

"She told me. That's great." Liam opened his case. "I'm glad it worked out. That wedding will be good promotion for you."

"It's a pretty fancy wedding for St. Cloud," Penny said.

"Political aspirations. They wanted to have it in Minneapolis, but Dani wants it in St. Cloud. It's about the only thing she got her own way." He handed her a stapled sheaf of papers.

"I thought you liked my business plan." Dismayed, Penny turned over the pages. "Three colors of high lighter?"

He moved over to sit next to her. "Now that I understand your business better, I have a couple suggestions." He used a gold pen to circle a paragraph. "What does this mean for your long-term growth? It seems stagnant."

"Stagnant? Is that like not scalable?" Penny glanced at the text and back at his face. Had he reduced the font size when he printed it?

"Stagnant. It sounds like you're planning to stay in one place without growing."

"Why not?" She avoided looking at the paper.

"You want to make more money, don't you?"

"No. Yes. I want enough money. Not rich, not poor. I want to meet my needs and put some in savings. Isn't that entrepreneurial enough for you?" Her voice rose in scale and pitch. She heard footsteps in the hall and Brian appeared in the doorway, frowning.

Penny clapped a hand over her mouth. "I'm sorry.

I shouldn't have said that. I do appreciate what you're doing. I've learned a lot. But I don't think I'm going to be what you want me to be." She gestured toward the paper. "Of course, I'd like to make more money. But I'm not going to be able to read your books or go through these papers with you. You know why?" She heard her voice rising and stopped to compose herself. "I can't read it. I have dyslexia. That's why I need people to help me with the paperwork. I'm sorry. I should have told you up front, but I get embarrassed about it."

She glanced at Brian. The warmth in his eyes encouraged her. She sat up straighter and met Liam's eyes. "I have the ability to read, but I can't do it with blocks of text or small writing. If you want me to read something, send it to me as a text document and I'll have the computer read it to me. I can't do it this way." She stood up. "I'm sorry, Liam. I should have told you. Can we just pick this up again next week? I need a break."

9

The pieces didn't fit together. Penny wanted to bang her head against the sewing machine. Straight lines. What could go wrong? At least it was just the sample block.

"I think I messed up."

Violet leaned over the ironing board, holding the piece she'd been pressing. "It looks okay."

Penny shook her head and laid the half-stitched pieces of fabric on the table. "Look. The line doesn't go right across the corner." She pushed the triangle open. "It's too big." She'd cut carefully, aligning the fabric with the pieces of tape Violet stuck to the ruler, so it must be her aunt's fault. Hopefully.

"No, it's just right." Violet pointed. "When you sew the next strip to it, that bit on the triangle seam allowance is caught in the seam and the finished triangle is the right size. A half-square triangle needs to be cut as a square seven-eighths of an inch bigger than the finished triangle."

Penny held up her hands. "You make it sound more like a math problem than a sewing project!"

"Well, it is. Otherwise the pieces don't fit together right, or the quilt is the wrong size. You do math in your work."

"As little as possible, and I use a calculator."

Violet laid her thin hand on Penny's shoulder. "I use a calculator, too, and a special software program for drafting quilts. Don't worry about it. Just keep sewing." Her gentle squeeze took the sting from the command.

"The triangles throw me. I don't know how you plan it out and make it fit together. My brain doesn't work that way."

"Mine does," Violet said. "I think it came from all those years working at the telephone company. I couldn't work with brides like you do, though. I'd probably tell them they look fat or they have no taste, or something like that. You have a way with people."

"Sometimes it's easier than others. I like the girl I'm working with now. I thought she was going to be snobby, when Liam described her to me, but she's not."

"It's short notice to make a wedding dress, though, especially when you're not finished with the house."

"I don't have much else going on, though, and it's fun to finally be working here. I have a couple consultations next week already." Penny positioned the fabric pieces under the needle. "I'll be glad when my apartment is ready. I'd thought I'd make one big move, with a grand opening, but I've just sort of migrated a bit at time, and now I've got my first real client here. It would be easier if everything was in one place." She chuckled. "Mom's moving her stuff into my old sewing room as fast as I take things out. She's looking forward to having a schoolroom."

"Your mother is the busiest person I know," Violet said. "Homeschooling."

Her huff was quieter than it had been five years

ago. It was hard to argue with results. "My grandparents built schools and made their children go. They moved to America to be American. The children weren't even allowed to speak Swedish."

Penny focused on sewing as her aunt related the familiar story. It was surprisingly hard to maintain a perfect quarter-inch seam allowance for what seemed like miles.

"My father was 18, but he went to school whenever he could. He said he went to take care of my mother, but I think he just wanted to learn English. By the time I was born, no one spoke Swedish anymore."

"Mm." Penny lifted the presser foot and pulled out the string of quilt pieces. If she was a swearing woman, this would be the time for a few choice expletives. Calico was such a solid fabric—not at all like satin or chiffon, so why was it so hard to keep straight?

"Now your cousin Marlys is paying for a class to learn it." Violet looked up at the suspended power bar. "This is nice, even for the little pieces."

"All done!" Penny stood and stretched. "You want some coffee? I need a break."

Violet checked her watch. "It's lunchtime. We could take our sandwiches out back."

"Sounds good." Penny tapped off the light switch as they left the room.

"It's strange to go through where walls used to be," Violet said, "and to have a door on the kitchen."

Penny reached around her to turn the knob. "It's not locked."

Her aunt entered the room slowly. "It's so white."

"It doesn't look too modern, does it? I want to continue the country chic theme, but it needs to look clean. I don't want the clients to think their dresses might get dirty."

"You never take the dresses in the kitchen! That's ridiculous."

"You'd be amazed at what brides think," Penny said. "I'm already having to overcome the stigma of having a bridal studio on a farm. I have to keep a balance between the style of the house and having it look modern and clean."

"Country chic." Her aunt shook her head. "I don't know where you get these things. I don't think this kitchen was any kind of chic when we lived here. It was clean, though."

"I'm sure it was." Penny took the filled cup and handed it to Violet. "I know your mom died when you were born. That must have been awful."

"I don't remember it, of course. She died a few days later, from a fever. Nowadays, they'd give her an antibiotic and she'd be fine."

"Aunt Kristina must have been more like a mother than a sister."

"She was all I knew." Violet sipped her coffee and walked to the sink to add water. "I went through a phase later, when I made up stories about how much my mother would have loved me, and all the things we would have done together."

"That's sad. But you had your dad and a lot of brothers and sisters."

"Oh, yes. I had Papa and Kristina and Linnea. And

the boys, for a while."

Penny perched on a stool. "Did you go to barn dances and ice cream socials? Dance around the maypole on Svenskarnas Dag?"

Violet raised her brows. "You have a romantic view of farm life. Mostly, we worked. We had church events, and we did go to the fair, but it was the pretty girls from town who did the dancing."

Penny smiled. "You were pretty. I've seen your pictures. You can't tell me you didn't have beaus."

"Well," her aunt said with a shrug. "There were a few boys who liked my pies, but Kristina kept me busy, and then there was work to do."

10

Penny shielded her eyes against the October sun. "Whatcha doing?" Brian matched the autumn landscape today, with his straw-colored hair and olive-green sweatshirt.

"Getting a cardboard box. I was digging a hole for that bush and found something."

"Over there where the dogs are buried?" She trailed him to his truck, clutching her warm coffee cup. "And you're going to put it in a box?"

"It's too small for a dog, and there was no marker on it. I think it's a wood box, but it's all wrapped up in an old quilt."

"A box!" Penny perked up. "Maybe it's the long-lost family treasure!"

"You have a family treasure?" Brian grabbed a box from the back of his truck and dumped its contents into the bed.

"Not that I ever heard of, but a box buried in the back yard must mean something exciting."

"Well, it could be a cat," he said. "A small cat. Did they ever have pet hamsters or something like that?"

"Yuck! I have no idea. Where'd you put it?"

"It's still there. I just dug around it and looked to see what it was." He gestured. "Want to see?"

"Yes! I'm still voting for treasure."

Brian pulled on his work gloves and used a garden spade to pry out the bundle. "I thought I hit a dog at first." He lifted a layer of the rotting cloth—it may have been white at some point—and revealed an edge of a wood box. "Too small for an animal. Too light to be gold. Maybe it's stuffed full of cash."

"Probably not," Penny said regretfully. "We come from a long line of poor but proud dairy farmers."

"Maybe your aunt knows something about it. I think there's carving on it." He poked at the decomposing fabric.

"It has to be something from her generation, and her parents built this house, so it must belong to our family."

Brian picked up the box. "I just hope it's not a family pet."

Aunt Violet peered into the cardboard box, hands covered in blue latex gloves as if ready to perform surgery on its contents.

"That's not a quilt. It's a blanket. It could have belonged to my mother. Her mother was a weaver, and we had blankets and rugs everywhere."

They all looked at the filthy remnants.

"The box might have been my father's," she continued. "He did woodworking—ordinary things for the house—but this is more decorative."

"I don't think the blanket will clean up," Brian said. "But I can wipe the mud off the box." Brian reached out and jerked his hand back when both women slapped it. "Hey! Just trying to be helpful!"

"Sorry." Violet touched the blanket with the tip of her blue finger. "I think we should try to save the blanket if we can, and, well... who knows what's in that box."

"Ashes come to mind," said Brian.

"They sure do." Penny regarded the box. It appeared to be about nine inches square. If it had hinges or a clasp, they were hidden in the dirt. "Maybe someone at the historical society knows how to clean it safely and has an idea what might be inside. If it's ashes, the person had to be cremated. Professionally, I mean."

Brian uttered a sound that was either gagging or laughter. Maybe both. She narrowed her eyes at him and continued. "There would be some kind of death record. There's no family cemetery here. Everyone's buried in the churchyard in town."

"Everyone that you know of," Brian said. "What if one of the graves there is empty or has someone else in it?"

"That's ridiculous." Penny glared at him and jerked a thumb toward her aunt, who was frowning at the box.

Brian flushed. "I know. sorry. It's probably some kind of family heirloom, buried for safekeeping, maybe during the war?"

Violet looked up. "Maybe. Maybe it's something that belonged to Hans or Karl. But I think I would have known about that. Or..." She winced. "I suppose it could be my first brother Hans."

They both stared at her, speechless.

"But it's too small for that, isn't it? He was buried in the churchyard. There's a headstone there. Anna, too, and if there had been another lost baby, they would have buried him or her there, too. At least, not in the yard, and there would have been a marker." She looked up, her face ashen. "Right?"

Penny hastened to reassure her. "Oh, yes, I am certain of it. Especially since it has the decorative carving. If someone went to so much trouble to carve a box and wrap it up, they would have made a marker."

Violet sank onto a chair. "Of course. It's just so strange."

"You had more than one brother Hans?"

"Oh yes. Two of them. It wasn't uncommon back then, if one baby died, to give that same name to the next one. It gets confusing for genealogists sometimes, because the church records don't indicate whether it was the first or second one—if you even realize there were two of them."

Penny tapped the edge of the cardboard box, relieved at her aunt's diversion. "Should we put this in the garage for now? Or we could take it to Dad, to see what he thinks." Pass the buck. But now that it was unearthed, it seemed callous to just dump it in the garage. "Maybe he knows something about it."

"Okay." Brian lifted the box. "I'll put this in my truck and drop it off at your parents' house on my way home."

"Thanks. I'll give Dad a call and tell him about it. I've got a client coming in about half an hour, but I'll be home by lunchtime. I don't want to miss the opening."

"Why don't you just take pictures of me?" Dani stepped onto the box.

"I'll do that, too, but first I'll sketch your body shape and make copies, so we can start drawing dresses. Put your feet six inches apart and lift your arms out to your sides. Perfect."

"How long have you been doing this?"

Penny opened the sketch pad and plucked a pencil from the jar. "Since I was a little girl and made fancy dresses for my Barbie dolls. They were always going to balls or getting married." She squinted at Dani and started drawing. "Then I started on dresses for my sisters and myself. I made some prom dresses for friends, and then when my best friend got married, she asked me to make her wedding dress. That was ten years ago, and it sort of took off from there."

"Your portfolios are gorgeous. You've done a lot of weddings in ten years. Isn't it hard to make a business of it, though—especially way out here?"

"Well," Penny said, "I've got this great business adviser."

Dani laughed. "He's pretty amazing, isn't he? He's so... alive."

"He's given me a lot to think about. The biggest advantage I have here is a low overhead. And it's what I want to do. My dad says that when we really want something, we make it happen, even when it seems impossible. My mother says, "With Christ, all things are possible. So how could I go wrong?"

"And this is what you wanted to do?"

"Can you turn around please? We have to design from the back, too. I took a career aptitude test before I went to college, and it said I should be a psychologist. So, I became a bridal gown designer."

"I can see how those would go together. You weren't interested in psychology?"

"I've never been good at school," Penny said. "I am good at designing and sewing."

"And you're dealing with stressed brides and mothers of brides. There's psychology in that."

"I like being able to listen to a bride and make her a perfect dress. Sometimes, they don't know what they want, or they have ideas that won't work. I don't make dresses that aren't just right for each bride."

"Have you ever turned anyone away?" Dani sounded intrigued.

"Not yet." Penny pulled out a new pencil. "But I'm a little worried about my sister. She wants to be Cinderella, with all her bridesmaids as the other Disney princesses."

"Let me guess. She's eight."

"No, she's 21 and engaged."

Dani chuckled. "Can I get an invitation to the wedding?"

"Probably. Lisa will invite everyone from the mailman to our third cousin twice removed. She's very soft-hearted. Okay, all done. I'll make copies and be right back."

Dani sat on the couch, resting her hand on an open

portfolio, when Penny returned. "I found one I really like."

"Which one?" Penny sat next to her.

"This one. It looks like a good compromise between the soft fabric and reality. Like it won't show every bulge and pimple. What do you think?"

Penny caught her breath. "I was just making sketches. Doodling around." She'd made a hundred sketches of that dress. "What do you like about it?"

"The skirt. It looks like a skirt you could dance in. And the princess seams. Princess seams work well for me."

"They're flattering for most people," Penny agreed. Dani and she were similar in shape and size. It would look good on her.

"What kind of fabric would you make it in?"

"A soft, barely off-white crepe de chine. It drapes, but it's heavier than the jersey knit of your last dress." She'd found it on one of her trips to the cities. It needed a moss green sash, for a summer wedding.

"I hated that dress. I'm glad it burned up. Do you think I could wear this one?"

"It's a good start," Penny said. "What would you change?"

Dani examined the drawing. "Well, maybe some kind of shawl or a little more shoulder cover, for a January wedding. And I'm still thinking I'd like a train if it could be bustled up."

Penny drew the dress—her dress—with the modifications. "You would also look good in a dress that fits and flatters your hourglass shape. Something like this." She paged through the book. "It has princess seams but it's more snug through the natural waist, and the skirt is more full."

"Okay, I can see me wearing that." Dani nodded. "It's a stiffer fabric, right?"

"Not stiff. And it would be comfortable." She smiled. "I only make comfortable dresses."

"I don't think getting it wet will hurt it. It's been buried in wet soil, not an airtight container, for who knows how long."

Violet was silent, but she didn't stop Constance from picking it up.

"Just warm water, no soap." Constance spoke soothingly, as if Violet was a child. "I won't scrub it or anything like that. We'll get the blanket loosened up so we can remove the box without damaging either of them."

Penny set the tub of warm water on the countertop. They looked a little silly standing around the kitchen island in elbow-length cleaning gloves, watching Constance gently massage the fabric.

"Is that cotton?" Penny touched it. "I thought it would be wool."

"Most of the older weavings were wool," Violet said, "but not all of them. It must have been made by my mother or grandmother. Kristina never used the loom. I think Linnea made a few rugs, but eventually Papa put it in the barn. Linnea took it when we cleaned everything out, but then she died, and I think Bonnie has it. It's an antique now."

Aunt Violet's chatter didn't conceal her anxiety. "There's a clasp. I hope it's not locked."

Penny doubted that the hinges or lock were still functional. "Dad said to let it dry, and he'll look at it. I think he just wants the fun of opening it himself."

"I hope it's fun," Constance muttered. She continued peeling away the blanket, wincing when the fabric broke. "I think we can save at least some of this, Violet, but it's a mess."

"I know."

"Got it!" Constance lifted the box and set it on a nest of towels. "I'll run some clean water in the bathtub to soak the blanket."

Penny and Violet looked at the box as if it might spring open. An antique jack in the box or morbid remains?

"It doesn't look moldy or broken," Penny said.

"It looks like something my father might have done. When Brian said it was carved, I didn't know, but it's just the top. He could have done that."

"Dad probably has tools to get it open without damaging it." Penny flexed her hands. "Or we could do it now if you don't want to wait."

"We can wait. If the box can be saved, I'd like to have it. Something from Mama, something from Papa." Violet didn't take her eyes from the mucky box. "An early Christmas gift."

"I told her I'd open it for her, but she just picked it up and left. In her car."

Penny dropped her phone on the table. "She's not answering, but she might still be driving, if she's going out to the house. Does she think it's some kind of deep, dark family secret?"

Her dad scratched his nose. "I don't think we're that kind of family."

"No one ever thinks that." Jeffrey Anderson squeezed his sister in a hug as he entered the room. "We're not that boring. Use your imagination. Maybe our great great great grandfather stole the crown jewels from Queen Ingeborg as she rode through their little village in Sweden. Maybe one of them created a fake Nordic rune stone and buried it there, knowing it would be dug up someday, just for fun. Maybe it's Great Aunt Kristina's recipe for lutefisk. Or Olof's recipe for moonshine. Maybe it's a treasure map. Maybe one of our 14 great uncles needed a place to bury a body, so when another one of them died, he had that one cremated and used the grave to bury his victim."

"You do have a revolting imagination, Jeffrey. Creepy. Maybe you get it from Aunt Violet and she's checking to see if there really are human remains in that box." Penny looked at her dad. "Do you think I should go check on her?"

Carl shook his head. "Violet's been through a lot in her years on earth. She can handle this."

"She must have been suspicious, though, or she wouldn't have taken off like that," Jeffrey insisted. "Maybe we do have skeletons in our closets."

Penny's phone rang. Brian. Leaving the men to speculate, she swiped across the screen to answer the call and headed for her bedroom.

"Hello."

"Hey, I've been waiting for a call." Brian sounded reproachful. Hurt? "I thought you were going to tell me what you found."

"We didn't open it. Dad was going to open the box when he got home, but Aunt Violet ran off with it. I guess she wants to open it in private. She's not answering her phone. I assume she's out at the house."

"Want me to run out and check on her?"

That was Brian. Penny smiled. "No, Dad says she's fine. She must have some idea of what's in there, though."

"Sounds like it, and she didn't want anyone else to see it. What do you think?"

Penny walked around a box of summer clothes and sat on the edge of her bed. "I honestly don't know. Jeffrey's full of ideas—everything from stolen jewels to recipes for lutefisk."

"Secret family recipe she's not willing to share?"

"None of us eat lutefisk," Penny said. "None of us. We each have one piece of pickled herring at Christmas and New Year's, to make Mom happy. That's as fishy as we get."

"You eat lake fish."

"You know what I mean." She flopped onto her back and gazed at the ceiling. "I can't imagine what's in there or—more interestingly—what she thinks is in there."

He made a thoughtful humming noise. "That's an interesting point. She knows something."

"You're as bad as Jeffrey."

"Impossible," Brian stated firmly. "No one's as bad as Jeffrey. So, if you can't satisfy my curiosity about the box, do you want to go out for an ice cream cone? We're not going to have many more warm evenings."

Penny looked around at the half-packed room. "Sure. That sounds great. Do you want to see if Angel and Sadie want to come along?"

"No, I don't. I was asking you, not the whole family. I've got some good news. Well, news anyhow."

She stood and grabbed a sweater from the closet. "Are you buying?"

"This doesn't qualify as a warm evening."

Brian put an arm around her. "Come on, Minnesota girl. We'll eat in the truck."

"You do know how to show a girl a good time." Penny waited while Brian adjusted the heat controls. "Are you ready to tell me your news? I've been patient."

"No, you haven't. You've asked me a dozen times already."

"Not a dozen. So, what is it?" She licked the edge of her already-dripping cone.

"My new boss is going to Arizona for the next three months."

"Oh, no!" Penny said. "Does that mean you still have a job or not?"

"I do, but not full-time yet. I'm going in on Monday morning to meet with him before he leaves. He says he has work for me to do, but it sounds like busy work I can do at home, and there's a series of videos he wants me to watch."

She couldn't see him roll his eyes in the dark confines of the truck, but she knew it happened. "Is this job really worth waiting for?"

"It is. It's exactly what I want to do, and it's here. Most of these companies are in the cities." Brian handed her a napkin. "I like this guy. He feels really bad about putting me off, but his surgery turned out to be more complicated and his wife wants him to recover in a warmer climate. If he wants to pay me to sit around and watch movies, I'm not going to complain."

"Oh." Penny turned in her seat, seeking his face in the dark. "You mean he's been paying you this whole time?"

"Yes." He chuckled. "I love you, Penny, but I couldn't afford to hang out and change your light bulbs and dig holes if I wasn't getting paid. I'd be out looking for another job."

Why had she thought she was paying him? Penny frowned at her melting cone, trying to remember what he'd said. She'd just assumed….

"You've been doing a lot more than changing light bulbs." She hadn't meant to take advantage of him. Grateful he couldn't see her face, she continued, "You probably ought to be using the time to work on your house."

"I am," he said. "You're not exactly a full-time job."

She could hear the smile in his voice, and she felt wretched. He'd done all of it as a favor, as a friend. Of course he had. He was Brian.

11

Violet

She hadn't been that dramatic since she was a teenager and Kristina made her milk the cow before she could leave for the Pearsons' barn dance. Violet clenched the steering wheel. Running off like this was silly and unnecessary. Whatever was in that box was… well, probably nothing. But if her father had made that box and wrapped it up in one of her mother's blankets, she wanted to know in private, without people around making comments and joking. Everything was a joke to them.

She squeezed her eyes shut and opened them again. Driving in the dusk, even when she wasn't blinded by tears, was risky. If she had an accident, everyone would be sympathetic and tactful and make suggestions about the wisdom of driving at her age. At her age. She was only 83 and in excellent health. Maybe she should have just sold the house and moved into a small home of her own, not dependent on her extended family. She was tired of being dependent.

Violet took a steadying breath and turned into the driveway. Carl had improved the driveway and front walk, and they'd added a porch with wide steps, but he hadn't made any big structural changes. Paint and new windows. The roof had been replaced years ago, after a tree had fallen in a storm. It looked pleasant and welcoming, but nothing like the home of her childhood. The house was a stranger now. Nothing but a little regret stirred in her. She just wanted to know what was inside the box, and she didn't want an audience.

Light flooded over her as she approached the front door. Startled, she grasped the handrail, nearly dropping the box. "Oh, Lord, please help me." The muttered prayer fell into the silent evening. She typed in the security code, feeling like a housebreaker. This wasn't her home anymore.

The green exit sign glowed on the blue walls, casting a spectral light on the white furniture. She walked through the house and turned on the kitchen lights. She refused to be spooked here.

She set the box on the scrubbed butcher block table and sank into a chair. Forty years ago, she could have tried using a hairpin to pick the lock, but her short curls no longer concealed anything useful.

Violet opened and closed drawers and cabinets in a futile search for tools. It wasn't a real kitchen anymore. Brian's toolbox, propping open the basement door, caught her attention. Perfect. She put on her readers and hunched over the box. Finesse and wiggling didn't do the job. She stabbed a screwdriver into the keyhole and wrenched it sideways. Nothing. This was a lot easier in the movies. Carl would have opened it without damaging it. Violet slid the screwdriver between the box and lid and pried it open. The lock bent, and she dragged it from the wood.

The tiny hinges held, and Violet had to run a knife around the edge of the box to break the seal of mud in the swollen wood. She used the knife to push the lid up and back, holding her breath, not blinking.

The box was filled with plaid fabric. Blue and white, or gray. Violet found a pair of gloves and dragged them on before removing the ball of fabric. No ashes or gold, but there was something wrapped up in the cloth. She set it on the table, carefully pressing the stiff fabric away from the treasure it cradled. The light item felt fragile, almost brittle, as she lifted it from its nest and placed it next to the box. The black metal piece was about the size of a juice glass, with a rod poked across near the bottom, like a tiny bird feeder.

Paper, folded and rolled up tightly, emerged from the open end. Violet gave it an experimental tug, and it slid out. Setting the paper aside, she picked up the dark metal tube and laid it on the palm of her hand. Tarnished silver? It had spikes on one end. She inhaled sharply, jerking her hand, nearly dropping the piece. She tipped it up and set it on its base on the table. She'd never seen one before, but she knew what this was, and it didn't belong in America.

Slowly, she reached for the paper, using her fingers to ease it open. Fine writing, in an unfamiliar masculine hand, covered both sides of the paper. She saw the signature first. Trembling, flooded with disbelief and excitement, Violet held her breath as she turned over the letter. Tears filled her eyes at the sight of the greeting. "Thank you, Jesus." Her whisper cracked.

Violet pushed the silver item away and smoothed

the curling paper on the table. This was the real treasure.

To my dearest Hilma,

I cannot sufficiently express my love to you on paper, through another man's writing, but I must commit a message before I have to leave. The war is coming, and they say it will end all wars forever. That is a lie. Nothing will end wars until our Savior comes back. The final battle is His and the outcome of that is already secure. But now, we go on killing each other to protect what is important. Nothing is more important to me than you.

I know how hard it was for you, coming to America as a young girl. The storms at sea—especially the last one, where you held my hand so tightly I thought it might break—were terrible. The community wasn't as easy as we had expected, or the land as easy to break. You were just a little girl, but you were brave and worked as hard as your mother did.

But even in your work, during the hardest times, you were like a star set into the night sky. You shone bright and fierce. In the daytime, you sparkled like the sunlight on the lake, stirred up by wind.

You always looked like light to me, even as a little girl, when you laughed because your mother braided your hair and it slid out every day. In the sunshine, your eyes absorbed all the blue from the sky. You were my light.

You left Sweden with only one regret, and still only had that one regret years later. Everything else was good and forward, but you regretted not being able to wear the *brudkrona*. It made you sad, and that seemed silly to you, but you had been so bold in everything else, not grumbling about anything else you had to leave behind. It was not silly to me. I wanted you to have it.

A friend helped me find a man who could make it. He is not a Swede and didn't know what it should be like, so I had to tell him and even draw pictures. He gave me work, so I didn't have to spend our seed money. Don't fear that I was foolish. If it had been necessary, though, I would have been just a little foolish, to get this gift for you.

It has no jewels, like the one in our church in Asele, but the smith was patient and cut it beautifully. I polished it, thinking of your delight, grateful that you are waiting for me. The silver will shine in the gold of your hair when we marry next month, but you always shine.

Perhaps God will bless us with daughters, and we will have this *brudkrona* to pass to them, or we can give it to the new church. But now, it is yours.

I wanted to save it and present it to you as a gift myself, on bended knee, as they do here in America with their wedding rings. I thought of serving it to you on a little pillow. But war is coming and my sweet Hilma, I sometimes fear that I may not make it back to you at all. I trust that I will, but I have decided to send this ahead.

After such a long friendship as ours, I was not certain that you would see me as a lover instead of a friend or brother. God was so good and faithful to open your eyes to see my love as it truly is—not just a friend, but a lover and husband. And I rejoice that you can wear this crown honestly on your wedding day with a full heart, as if we were back in Sweden, but in a better place now. God willing, we will grow prosperous and have many children to share our love. But whether in wealth or humble estate, I am entirely yours.

Your soon-to-be husband, Johannes

12

I don't know. She's not saying." Penny glanced at her aunt, who stood chatting placidly with the pastor. The old woman leaned on her cane, looking deceptively fragile. "She didn't even bring the box back. She just says, 'I know what it is and I'm not going to talk about it right now.' She doesn't say when she's going to tell us or give us any hints."

"And it's making you crazy." Brian grinned. "You're used to people talking to you. Baring their souls. Then you make them feel better."

"Me? I'm not like that."

"That's exactly how you are." Brian intercepted a fleeing preschooler and turned him back toward his mother. "It's a good thing."

"It doesn't sound like a good thing. Anyhow, Violet isn't talking. It's worse than not knowing what was in the box."

"I bet Jeffrey's loving that."

"Ha. Eighteen-year-old Jeffrey was told to leave the table at dinner the other night. He kept coming up with theories and asking her if he was right. Dad finally told him to go to his room. You should have seen Jeffrey's face." Penny snickered. "It was awesome."

"It's more mysterious now than it was when we first found the box. There's my ride. Dad's helping me put in windows today." Brian opened the car door and slid inside. "Call me if you find out."

Penny dropped the wet rag into the tote and watched Liam's SUV sweep into the driveway. She'd worried all morning, afraid he wouldn't come back after her tantrum. She'd been rude and unfair. She should have told him at their first meeting. He couldn't help her if he didn't know her limitations. No, not limitations. Just some things that needed workarounds. Everyone learned and worked differently, right?

He was already inside by the time she got downstairs. "Hello! Did you know your front door is open? I'm pretty sure brides don't want flies buzzing around their beautiful gowns."

She relaxed under his teasing. "Thanks. Did you close it?"

"I did. And I brought coffee." He held up the carrier. "I got you a mocha, since I didn't know what you like. It's my favorite, so if you're a coffee hater, I'll drink it myself."

"No way!" Penny took the cup. "We just can't have anything but water in the design studio or workroom. You want to sit out front?"

"That works. It's nice out, for November."

Penny sat on the step and Liam dropped down beside her. "Maybe you should get some chairs for the porch."

"A porch swing and rocking chairs to complete the

old lady seamstress image?"

He leaned back to look at the porch. "You could do something more modern, but a porch swing sounds good."

"We have a patio out back, where Aunt Violet can see the river." Penny sipped her coffee. "She can't, of course, but they could when she was a girl."

"I'm sure it's more private back there. You don't get a lot of privacy when you live above your shop."

"It's not like a grocery store in the city." Penny said. "There's not much traffic out here. Of course, you'd think I was opening a concert venue, according to the zoning board."

"Remember—zoning and insurance rule the world."

She chuckled. "I've learned that much."

"I want to apologize for upsetting you the other day."

She bit her lip at the abrupt statement. "I was just thinking that I'm the one who should apologize. I should've told you about it from the start. I get defensive."

"Understandable, but I could have been more helpful if I'd known in advance."

"I think that's part of why I've resisted the marketing stuff. It's a lot of reading and writing."

"You could hire someone. I read some articles on dyslexia. They said dyslexic business owners are good at delegating. They focus on the aspects they do best."

"Liam!" Penny turned to face him. "I'm impressed that you took the time to research me, but—"

"To research dyslexia," he interrupted, "so I'd be better prepared to help. I didn't mean to offend you."

"You did offend me! You're lumping me into a disability group." She knew he wasn't, though. Liam meant well.

"No, I'm not! I was talking about something that's an asset to an entrepreneur—delegating responsibility. Everything I read—every interview with dyslexic businessmen—mentioned that. I'm sorry if I offended you. I didn't mean to."

She deflated. "No, I'm sorry. Ninety-nine percent of the time, I don't care if people mention it, but sometimes things just rub me the wrong way. Brian says I get snarky to compensate for it. You didn't do anything wrong. I'm really grateful you went to so much trouble for me."

"Not just for you. I found it interesting. It makes you think about illiteracy differently. I guess if you can't see the words, you're not going to learn to read."

"Right." Penny kicked a stray leaf off the step. "There's more to it than that, but that's what it boils down to. But we were talking about marketing. I watched your video, and I can see where I'm messing up, but I don't know what to do about it. I really don't want to be driving all over the place doing bridal fairs, and they're expensive. Advertising in magazines is even worse. It seems like word of mouth would be the best way to get new people."

Liam pushed his hair behind his ear. "Theoretically. But weddings are a once-in-a-lifetime thing and you only need one dress. I don't know if that's supportable. According to Dani, bridal fairs and wedding websites like The Knot are the way to go. You have to use social media, and you have to have a better website."

"I don't have time to do those things, even if I knew how."

"Find someone. Come to a chamber meeting and talk to some of the people there. Local networking is important."

Penny groaned. "Liam, I have nothing in common with other local businesses. They're all about tourism—and some like your company. Nobody's interested in a girl who makes wedding dresses. Like you said, this isn't my market."

Liam stuck out his dimpled chin. "It's still important." He handed her a checklist.

He'd printed it in a large dyslexic font. Penny smiled. He really was a very nice guy—and persistent. She'd asked for a mentor, and Liam was going to mentor her whether she liked it or not.

"It occurred to me a while ago that my father might have been dyslexic." Her aunt pinned pieces of fabric together, not looking up as she spoke. "I don't think he could read or write well. It could have been the language; he didn't learn English until he was 18. I only ever remember Kristina and my brothers doing the farm paperwork."

"Really? My dad said he had trouble reading when he was younger, but it got better. None of my other siblings have it, and it's supposed to be hereditary."

"Olof never learned to read," Violet said. "He was always in trouble at school and in town. He worked on the farm, though, like Papa and did fine there."

"I didn't realize that." Penny positioned the fabric, muttered a prayer, and stepped on the foot pedal. "I'm just glad they can diagnose it now. I felt stupid before I found out what it was, and then I was relieved to have an excuse for avoiding work. Mom didn't put up with that, though. At first, she was determined to fix me. That was before you came, I think. She tried every kind of training and new theory. I have glasses in every color of the rainbow, overlays, keyboard adapters, headsets, special pencils and ruled paper. My computer is loaded with special software and half a dozen fonts specifically designed for dyslexia."

"She had just taken you out of school when I went to live with your grandma. I remember how upset she was, but you know she felt guilty for not realizing it herself."

Penny yanked the thread from the top of the machine. "I need to rethread this. She couldn't have known. She trusted the teachers when they said I was fine. Besides, she had six kids in nine years, and two of them were twin boys."

"And you worked hard to make sure no one knew you had a problem," Violet said. "I remember you always wanted people to read to you."

"And I went to the Michaels' house after school every day and got Faith and Brian to help me with my homework."

Violet set a pile of freshly pressed quilt pieces next to the sewing machine. "Olof wasn't that clever. He just didn't try, and he got in trouble. Back then, we didn't have any idea."

Penny handed her aunt the piece she had just sewn. "Is this right? It looks funny with that strip too short."

"It's not too short. Do the other side just like this one, but on the opposite corner." Violet plucked a pin from the cushion and aligned the pieces.

"Okay, but I have to say, it doesn't make sense to me."

"It's a math thing. I could explain it, but I think you'll see it on your own if you do it a few times. It really does make sense."

Penny shrugged and set the fabric under the presser foot. "That's how most sewing is for me. Eventually I learned to identify things. I hardly ever set in the wrong sleeves anymore."

"You're good at what you do because you see the big picture and then put it together in a series of smaller pictures."

"I think that's why I liked sewing when I was so young." Penny pulled the fabric out of the machine and thumbed it open. "Those patterns are all pictures. I didn't have to read the directions to succeed."

"That's not how everyone learns, though," Violet said. "Most people find those patterns frustrating. You see them, and they make sense to you."

"They work for me," Penny agreed. "You know, it's sad to think of all the people who had dyslexia before it was recognized as a learning problem. My mom gave me a poster with names of all these famous people with dyslexia, but they were the exceptions. Most people are more like Uncle Olof."

Violet snipped a thread and set the block on the rapidly growing pile. "I recently came across a letter my father wrote to my mother before they were married. He'd dictated it to someone—probably a pastor—who wrote it out for him."

"Really!" Penny stopped sewing and turned to look at her aunt. "I didn't know you had old letters."

"Oh yes, a few of them. It was expected, back then. Soldiers seemed to spend as much time writing letters as they did fighting." Violet shook her head. "That sounds bad. But we did receive letters from Hans and Karl. Karl always wrote to me separately, and I have all of his letters."

"So, they couldn't have had dyslexia."

"I don't think so," said her aunt. "The letters were easy to read, even though I was only eight or ten at the time. Hans died when I was nine, and Karl was a year after that."

Penny stared at her. "You know, Violet, it sounds like you've had a horrible life."

Violet chuckled. "I guess it does, when I talk about it like that, and that was indeed a horrible time. But there were good times, and it got easier as I got older. It helped that my father was a staunch Christian."

"Staunch! That's an odd word to describe a Christian."

"Well," Violet closed her eyes in concentration.

"He believed in God and he was stubborn about it. Through all the tragedies he endured, he just kept persevering."

"Stoic?" Penny suggested.

"No, that sounds too defeated. I was a baby when my mother died, and there were babies who died before I was born, and then the boys died in World War Two, but my papa was still a believer when I was old enough to know him. He was hardworking and there were hard times that made him angry or sad, but he still trusted God to get him to an eternal life in a better place."

Penny picked up another set of strips. "Were all of your family Christians?"

"Yes. At least, as far as I know. We had family devotions after dinner, but then the boys were gone, and Papa just prayed. He didn't read from the Bible. Now I wonder if he could read at all. The Bible had tiny print, too. He'd memorized passages, as a boy in Sweden and at church here, but I don't think he could read it for himself. Not really." Violet looked out the window. "Poor Papa."

13

Penny regarded her new client with suspicion. "Did Liam send you?" The email signature, according to Aunt Violet, proclaimed Brittany Green to be a social media marketing consultant.

"No." The girl raised her brows. "I don't know a Liam. At least, not one over the age of six."

"Okay." Penny felt herself flush. She'd been certain this was a ploy to get her to improve her online presence. Now she looked like an idiot. "Liam Ferra's my business adviser, and he likes to send brides my way." One, anyhow. Not exactly a lie.

"You made a dress for one of my friends a few years ago. I was a bridesmaid. She gave me your name." Brittany slid out of her coat and handed it to Penny. "I found your website."

Penny wrinkled her nose. "I know it's terrible. Come on inside. You did say your wedding is next Christmas, right? Not this one."

"Oh, yeah. I wouldn't even ask you to try for this year." As soon as she was seated, Brittany opened her purse and pulled out a sheet of paper. "I know what I want."

"Good." Wary, Penny sat and smiled encouragingly. "What do you have in mind?"

"This." Brittany shoved the paper at Penny. "I've

dreamed of this my whole life." The girl stared earnestly at Penny. "Every Christmas, I've watched the movie and dreamed of having a wedding like this one." She pointed at the grainy picture.

Torn between laughter and incredulity, Penny asked, "Even the choir and ballerinas?"

Brittany shook her head. "No choir. But I have a few nieces in ballet classes, and they love tutus. I may have to compromise on the toe shoes, though. They'd probably trip and break their ankles."

"The little boys in Santa suits?"

The girl giggled. "My little brother said he'd do it for a hundred dollars."

Penny gazed at her in consternation. She was serious. "Is it an indoor wedding? I mean, those dresses…" She tapped the picture. "That's going to be hot."

"It doesn't matter. This is my dream. And we can't have a Christmas wedding outdoors."

Penny played with the mechanical pencil. Would this be the first bride she had to turn away? But the girl had dreamed of a White Christmas wedding. Penny had designed her own wedding dress at twelve years old. Of course, her dress was white instead of red, and it didn't have fur trim. She tried again.

"It's a great movie. Not many brides wear red, though, and like I said, it's going to be hot, especially with the fur trim. And the bridesmaid matching you? Are you just having one?"

Brittany nodded. "Yes, my best friend."

Penny wondered who was paying for the dress.

Did her mother know what Brittany had in mind? She pulled the picture toward herself. "Can I hang on to this? I'll do up a few sketches and we can talk about it some more. Are you available on Monday?"

The girl seemed reluctant to leave. "Can you do it? Both dresses, and the little girls."

"Probably." Penny picked up the picture. "It's different. I'd like to make some sketches."

"But I want it just like that!" Brittany stood, hooking her purse over her shoulder. "Just like the movie."

"It should be doable. If you come back on Monday, I'll have some designs ready for you. We can talk and then sign a contract if we have an agreement. You're welcome to bring your mom and bridesmaid with you."

If the mother was on board, it might be a fun project. Penny waved goodbye and went back inside.

"Hey there. Don't knock me down."

Penny stopped short and looked up to see Brian on a ladder, changing light bulbs. "What are you doing?"

"Your aunt said these bulbs were too blue. I'm putting soft whites up instead. Why didn't you tell me?"

"I forgot. I'd think about it when I turned the lights on and then forget about it until the next time."

Brian nodded his head at the departing car. "Was that Coach Green's daughter?"

"Oh, I hadn't made the connection. I suppose it is. Her name is Brittany, and she wants a White Christmas wedding."

"Did you tell her you're not God?"

"What?"

"You can't make it snow," Brian said with exaggerated patience. "Sometimes we don't have snow on Christmas."

Penny laughed. "No, not that kind of White Christmas. The movie."

"What movie?"

"White Christmas," Penny said. "You know… Bing Crosby and Danny Kaye. Rosemary Clooney."

"I know the song."

"You must have seen the movie."

Brian shook his head. "We didn't see a lot of movies growing up."

Oh, right. "Faith and I watched it at my house. It's a great movie."

"I'd watch it with you." He climbed down the ladder and handed her the rejected light bulb. "If it's that famous, it's bound to be online."

"Probably, but it's an old movie. A mushy musical. No car chases or fights."

He looked offended. "My tastes are not limited to car chases and fights. Besides, it'll be a cheap date." He looked around. "We could watch it here."

A cheap date? A date with Brian? At one time, when she was seventeen, that would have thrilled her, but he'd just gone away to school with a brotherly hug at his farewell party. It wasn't even a hug—more of a slap on the back. They were back to their childhood friendship now, and it was nice.

"What do you think?"

Penny started at the question. "Sure. I'll make popcorn."

Brian picked up the remote and hit the pause button. "She wants this for her wedding?"

"Yeah. I'm thinking about it."

"But… the Santa suits."

"She said her brother would do it if…" Penny's mouth fell open. "The men are in Santa suits, too. You don't think…"

"Impossible. No man on earth would get married in a Santa suit—especially a shiny, sparkly Santa suit with all that fur. The kids look miserable. That last one looks like she's ready to cry." He gestured toward the computer screen. "And what's with all the guys with the candles?"

Penny grabbed the remote and resumed the movie. "It's almost over. Just watch."

She sighed with contentment as the familiar song played, the snow fell, and all the people rose to greet each other and shake hands. "I love this movie."

"But where was the wedding?"

She stared at him. "Well, I guess I was thinking that was the wedding scene."

Brian shook his head. "No wedding. I was watching for a wedding. That was just a song and dance number."

"You're right! I wonder why we always think of that as a wedding scene."

"It's a romantic scene. Nice dress, but… red? That would be different." He started to prop his feet on the table and then dropped them to the floor with a guilty look at Penny. "Sorry."

"Rosemary Clooney carried it off, but she's a lot older than Brittany Green. The orchestral accompaniment helped, too. I don't know. It's an appealing project, but I've got this policy about never letting a bride wear a dress that's not right for her." Penny nestled into the couch and put her feet on the table.

"According to who?"

"What?" Penny stopped licking the salt off her fingers and looked at Brian.

"I mean, she seems to think it's perfect. That's what matters, right?"

"No. Not for me. This is my reputation, Brian. I have to have a really good reputation to get brides willing to come up from the cities and pay my prices. I knew that, but Liam's really been harping on it. He talks about branding and marketing like they're more important than the actual work."

"Are you a brand now? Like Pepsi or Chevrolet?"

"Not yet, but I guess I need to be. Liam says if I'm going to make enough money to stay afloat forever, Penny Anderson Designs needs to be exclusive and expensive. It's all about the image." She shook her head. "He even wants me to use the word 'bespoke' in my advertising, but I can't do it. It's pretentious."

"And incorrect usage," said Brian. "So, what kind of advertising are you going to do?"

"I don't know. They have big bridal shows in the cities every year. Bridal Cons. Liam says I should go to those and talk to brides. He says I'm good at that."

"You are. Do you have to pay to participate in

those things?" He didn't sound convinced.

"Oh, yeah. But it might be worth it. It's my target market."

"Does Liam say that, too?"

Penny bristled. "No need to be sarcastic about it. I want to be successful, and I'm not going to make it on local brides. I don't want to be a dressmaking machine, just turning out ordinary dresses. I like the designing part, collaborating with the bride or whoever I'm sewing for. I like to be creative."

"You've always been creative, Penny. That's what made you so much fun when we were kids. Even though Faith was three years older than you, she just tagged along doing whatever you were doing."

"You were usually around, too."

"I didn't have a lot of friends. You were the most interesting person I knew."

Penny felt heat in her cheeks. "I didn't feel interesting. I felt like I was always asking you for help. Like I was a nuisance."

"That was a bad idea. Your parents were mad when they found out. And they should have been! I didn't do you any favors, in the end. Maybe if they'd diagnosed your dyslexia earlier…"

"Nothing would have changed. I was turning in perfect homework and unable to do the work in school. It turned out good in the end. Mom was so mad the school hadn't caught it that she started homeschooling, and that was great. Besides, she blamed me for cheating more than she blamed you for helping me."

"It seemed like a good idea at the time," Brian said.

"And I would have done anything for you. I was like a lovesick puppy."

"A lovesick puppy?" Penny asked. She didn't remember it that way. She scrambled to her feet. "That was fun. Thanks for watching it with me."

"What are you going to do about Brittany?" Brian zipped his jacket.

"I have an idea."

14

Penny bent close to the sewing machine and guided the fabric under the needle. "This part is the worst, right? It's not just the long bias seam; it's hard to keep sewing straight over all those lumpy seam allowances." She pulled the block out of the machine and lifted it for her aunt's inspection.

"It looks fine." Violet laid it on the ironing pile. "You're never going to be perfect. We can steam it into shape or ease in the fullness if necessary. That's why I like to work with fabric instead of wood. It's more forgiving."

"Cotton is a little more forgiving than most bridal fabrics," Penny conceded. "Satin is the worst, especially in a smooth pattern. It has to be perfect—or as close as I can get. I used to think velvet would be the worst, but that's just a matter of cutting it right." She held up the next block. "Here's another one. I think it's a little better."

"You're doing just fine. It must be less stressful than making wedding dresses, with that expensive fabric and high-strung brides."

"Right now," Penny said, "this is more stressful. I missed the bottom layer." She picked up the seam ripper and began picking at stitches. "It is hard when they're high-strung. I mean, I know it's the most important day of their lives—or they think it is—but they get so stressed out about the whole wedding. They don't get to just enjoy it." She pulled the two pieces apart and handed them to her aunt. "Can you iron those, please?"

"Sometimes it seems like their mothers are the ones making them stressed-out. Here you go."

Penny took the pieces and realigned them. "What brides don't understand is that a wedding dress is really just a costume. The wedding is an event—a performance. They're onstage all day and then the costume gets packed away. It may be worn by someone else in another show someday, but it's served its purpose: the bride looked great in the wedding pictures."

"A wedding shouldn't be a show," Aunt Violet snapped. "It's supposed to be a sacred ceremony."

"Oh, come on, Aunt Violet. Some weddings are. They all are, theoretically, but when it comes right down to it, it's a performance and a party. People spend tens of thousands of dollars on a wedding."

"That's pretty cynical, for someone who's in the business of making bridal gowns."

"Oh, I'm more than happy to collect my share of that money." Penny sat up and stretched. "I know some weddings can be a meaningful Christian union and still cost a lot of money because it's just expensive. A venue, meals, flowers and pictures, clothing… it just adds up."

"Your Grandpa and Grandma Anderson had a lovely Swedish wedding. Maria's family didn't give up all the old traditions like our parents did."

"Neither did my mom's grandparents," Penny said. "That's why we have Santa Lucia and herring and all the rest of it."

"It's a good thing," Violet said. "You should know

about your ancestors."

"That's why you make the quilts, right?"

"Yes, and the little books to go with them." Violet handed a block to Penny. "This one needs to be redone."

Penny took it and started picking stitches. "I didn't know you wrote books." It was the first time in her life Penny had seen a positive consequence of her dyslexia. At least she wouldn't be expected to carry on that pursuit.

"There's all the genealogical records, too," Violet said. "All of that's online, but I've printed out copies, just in case."

Just in case the internet disappeared. Penny hid a smile. "It sounds like a big project."

"It is, but you'd be amazed what you can find online. The churches kept detailed records of everyone's lives. And what they missed, the government here picked up."

"It's all online?"

"It is. And now, people are doing DNA tests, too."

"Oh, right. They find out they're really French when they thought they were Native American."

Her aunt shook her head. "Those are just for entertainment. Real genealogists are doing the kind of tests you see on crime shows. They're finding people they're related to all over the world."

"Or finding out they're adopted?" Penny asked.

"Sometimes."

"And you're using quilts to tell the stories?"

"I make blocks," Violet said, "and sew them into quilts when they're ready."

"What do you mean?" Penny pushed her chair

back and looked at her aunt. "You just make blocks? Like these?" She nodded at the stack on the ironing board.

"Yes. I work ahead. I have a lot of quilts to do, and they all overlap. Your parents' quilt has blocks for you, and I'll make more for your children. You'll have some of the same blocks on your quilt, and more blocks for your children and grandchildren."

Her quilt? Oh boy. Maybe she could use it for picnics. "Are you making quilts for everyone? How many have you made?"

"Ten so far, not counting a few smaller ones. Your Aunt Molly made a couple of them, too, before her hands got bad. Those include a lot of detail about her own family, because she was making them for her own kids."

"Ten!"

"But I have blocks for a dozen more." Violet set the iron on its rack. "If I don't make them for everyone, people will be fighting over them when I'm gone."

Not likely. Penny felt a wash of shame at her reaction. This was important to Violet and not something to be mocked.

"So, how does it work? You make blocks for each person in the family? And every quilt includes all the family members? How do you stop? I mean, Mom and Dad only have one grandchild so far, but there will be more. And my aunts and uncles and cousins. Everyone keeps reproducing."

"That's why I make blocks. I know I can't get it all, but I can add onto them with applique and embroidery later. I've completely finished mine." Her voice was matter-of-fact.

"That's morbid," Penny said. "It sounds like you're saying your life is over."

Her aunt smiled. "No, because I can't record my death. Someone else will have to do that. Mine includes my grandparents and parents and how they immigrated from Sweden, and all my siblings and their children."

"It must be huge!"

"Just the right size for me. It's the family God gave me, after all."

Aunt Violet was making divinely inspired quilts. "So, do you just start the quilts and then wait until something new happens? And make a bunch of blocks for each event, so you can put them in different quilts?"

"Yes."

Penny grinned. "Are you making quilts for the guys? Like Uncle Gary? Separate quilts for each wife?"

"That does complicate things." Violet sighed. "So far I'm just making blocks."

"Don't want to commit, huh?" Penny chuckled. "Neither does Uncle Gary." She felt instant remorse at the regret on her aunt's face. "I'm sorry. That was tacky."

"In a way," Violet said slowly, "a quilt is a good illustration of situations like that. Your Uncle Gary's life has been complicated. There are a lot of pieces in it, some big and some small, some bright and pretty colors, and some dark pieces, too. Some of the pieces are squares, some rectangles or triangles. It isn't going to be a neat quilt like this one, but we don't know. It might end up being a beautiful scrap quilt, or it might not be very pretty at all, with uneven stitching, points that don't match up and colors that clash. But it will be a quilt. His quilt."

"But what if he doesn't want all the pieces to be in his quilt, reminders of things he doesn't want to remember? Or regrets?"

Aunt Violet walked across the room and sat in one of the upholstered chairs. "Like I said, most of Gary's is just blocks. That's how I do it. I make blocks, and when I have enough blocks to make a row, I sew them together and add them to the bottom of what I already have. Like a book. You start at the top of the page and read left to right and downward."

"Interesting." Penny meant it. "It's like a scrapbook."

"Yes. You work on it as you go. I have a couple blocks for you, but I can't write your whole story until you live it out. I make the blocks now because I have to stay on top of it in bits and pieces, or it will never get done."

Penny didn't point out that Violet would be dead long before most of their lives would be lived out. She wasn't providing the older woman with an opportunity to ask her to take it over.

"My favorite block is the one I made for your great great grandmother, Brita. She was 43 when Papa set off for America. She had other children there and wouldn't leave. Every Sunday, after church, we wrote letters to her. Her pastor translated them for her. She wrote back in Swedish, and our pastor translated for us. Her letters always seemed to talk about her goats and our cousins we didn't know. I remember being jealous of those cousins. I didn't have a grandmother or mother." Violet fell into silence.

"And I'll have a block about her on my quilt." So much for using it as a picnic blanket. The thing would have to go into a cedar trunk and become a family heirloom.

"Yes." Violet seemed to shake off the memories. "The quilts overlap generations and extended families. There's just one block on yours for your great uncle Elim and his wife and their children, and they only have one block to represent all of you, but it's important to have that block."

"So, your quilt..." Penny came to a stop. Her aunt had never married.

"It's mostly about my nieces and nephews, siblings, parents, grandparents and great grandparents."

"And you have fabric scraps from all of them?"

"Oh, no! Not all of these are actual scraps from people's clothing," Violet said. "Most of them are just representative. Sometimes I see a piece of fabric that reminds me of someone, so I buy it and cut it up. It's all in the Rubbermaid totes."

"Well, it sounds very interesting," Penny repeated. "I hope you are around to make quilt blocks for generations to come."

"Probably not," said her aunt, "and that's all right. God's worked it out. If He wants quilts, He'll send a quilter."

15

Dani's dimples and bright eyes gave her a pixie-like charm. "I know my appointment's not for two hours, but I needed a ride, and Liam was on his way out here, so if you don't mind me hanging out on the porch while you do your business, I can use my phone to answer some emails."

"Or play Word Spin or Box Drop or Dragon Kill," Liam teased.

"Hey… nothing wrong with a game now and then." Penny smiled at Dani. "It's pretty cold out. You're welcome to stay out here or come inside or whatever you want. I think today's agenda mostly consists of nagging me to get a new logo and update my website."

"Nagging!" Liam put a hand on his chest as if she'd wounded him. "I'm a consultant. I advise, not nag. And a mentor, too, so I think you're supposed to be respectful and admire my business acumen."

"I do, I do."

Dani interrupted. "Acumen? Who uses a word like acumen? It seems to me that you're just bossy and enjoy telling her what to do. Feeding your already plump ego."

"Plump ego? That's better than acumen? It seems to me that you enjoy being rude."

Penny raised her brows. If Dani wasn't already engaged, she'd have thought their banter a sign of budding romance. "I was kidding. Liam doesn't nag. He just sort of... exhorts."

"Exhorts?" They spoke at once. Maybe they didn't hear that word often. It was probably what her brothers called Christianese.

"Never mind. I'm ready to be mentored."

Liam followed her inside and brooded as she fetched her laptop and returned to the consultation area. "I don't know why she wants to marry that guy. He's not at all her type. She's fun and happy. He's ambitious and only cares about how she can be an asset in his career."

So, there was an attraction, at least on Liam's part. Penny sat on the couch and opened the computer. "It's hard to know what people see in each other."

"He's pretty obvious."

"Liam, I'm not going to gossip about Dani's fiancé."

"No, sorry. I didn't mean that. She must love him, or she wouldn't be engaged to him. I just don't know what she sees in him."

"Liam! Can we talk about my shortcomings as an entrepreneur?"

He chuckled. "I don't think of you that way. You just need to start applying the things you already know."

"I've been so busy! I didn't expect to take on any new clients before I'd officially opened the shop, and I underestimated how much work the renovations would be, and I'm supposed to be helping my aunt with her quilt." Penny hunched her shoulders. "And it's easy for me to push the business things to the bottom of my priority list. Even Aunt Violet commented on it. She's supposed to be my office person, but I'm not giving her anything to do."

"Make lists. Get organized. You didn't expect to open your business so soon, but here you are... open! What about the social media? I don't suppose your aunt's interested in that."

"No," Penny said. "She still thinks the internet is just a passing fad. She uses it for genealogy research and prints everything out, so she doesn't lose it. She doesn't get the cloud storage idea."

"You could ask Dani to help you with it. She was doing all the social media marketing for the sorority before she quit." He sounded so disingenuous that Penny almost believed it was a spontaneous suggestion.

"Liam, she's planning a wedding. Do you have any idea how time-consuming that is?"

"It would give her something fun to do."

"Liam!" Penny swatted his arm. "I can't ask her to do that."

"I could."

"No," she said firmly, "you can't. Are we going to do something productive today?"

"Okay, okay. By the way, I sent you links to those articles I mentioned. Did you know Steve Jobs was dyslexic? And Steven Spielberg, too. Apparently, dyslexia develops a different skill set, like being able to see the bigger picture and not getting tied up in the steps to get there. You hire people for some things, so you can focus on the things you do best. They say dyslexic businessmen take more risks and just sort of believe they can do whatever they want." Liam pointed at her. "I think that's how you're seeing your business."

"It's really nice of you to go to so much trouble," Penny said. "Thank you."

He shrugged, a pink hue rising under his olive skin. "I just wanted to understand, and it was interesting. Most people with dyslexia tend to outgrow it, but you didn't?"

"I'm better than I was. It mostly feels like a vision problem now. Mostly."

"If I'm going to help, I need to know how you see your business. And I think I have a better understanding now. It was really interesting reading. Every article said that dyslexic people tend to be good at creative problem solving. I could see that in you."

Penny relaxed against the cushions. "Did your research also tell you that dyslexic kids tend to get bullied at school and have depression or low self-esteem? They either crash and burn, or they excel, usually depending on whether or not they have support from parents and teachers. My dyslexia was diagnosed later than usual, because I developed some sneaky ways to look like I was keeping up with my classmates. Ways that included lying and cheating. Creative problem solving. I even got Brian to do my homework for me and read my books to me."

"Brian? The guy who works here?"

"He doesn't work here." Penny squirmed. "At least, he doesn't get paid. He just... likes to help."

Liam raised his brows. "Help? He's here every time I am. Does he have a real job?"

"Yes! He's an electrical engineer, and he has a job in Princeton. He's just on a sort of leave right now, while the owner's out of town." She regarded Liam. "You know, Dani's probably getting cold out there. Maybe we should cut this short, so she and I can have her design session early."

Liam opened his car door. "Are you sure an hour will be enough time?"

"Yes, plenty. We're just finalizing a pattern today," Penny said.

"Well, call if you need me to come back early." He looked at Dani. "You have my number if you need me."

Penny and Dani waved and watched as he turned onto the highway.

"Have you ever met anyone so... alive?"

Penny looked at the other woman in surprise. "That's a good way to describe him. Handsome, too, if you like long curly hair, big brown eyes, a cleft chin and dimples. Tall, dark and handsome, that's Liam."

Dani laughed. "Yes, it is."

"Are you ready?" Penny held the door open. "I made some more sketches and brought out a few fabric swatches for you."

"I have a picture, too."

"Oh, good. I'd like to see it." Penny slid into her seat and reached across to take the single sheet of paper.

"I don't know if it's possible, but those are some of the details I liked." She leaned forward eagerly.

Penny looked from the drawing to the girl's face. "Dani, this is exactly like the sketch you looked at last week." The sketch of her own dress.

"That must be a sign, right? You drew it, I drew it, and I think it would fit well. I'm good with this one."

It would be perfect for her. Penny took a deep breath and exhaled. "Okay, let's look at fabrics."

"Don't you think it's a good choice?" Dani asked.

"I do." Penny forced a chuckle. "It's always been my favorite. I designed it when I was twelve years old."

"You designed it for yourself!" Dani turned the paper around to look at it again. "Do you mind making it for me? I don't want to use it if it's a problem."

"No," Penny said. "It's not a problem at all. I've just never had anyone notice it before or want anything like it. You and I are pretty similar in shape, so it should work well for you. After all, I might not ever have occasion to wear it, and it would be a shame if I never got to make it."

"You don't think you'll get married someday?"

"Maybe, maybe not." Penny stood up and retrieved the fabric swatches from the worktable. "I always imagined this one. And a green sash."

"I don't think mine should have a separate color, do you? My bridesmaids are in champagne, so I could just use this same fabric for the sash."

"That works. It will be beautiful. "Why did she feel so reluctant? There was nothing wrong with making it twice, if she did get married someday, and she liked Dani. She pulled out the bolt she'd bought years earlier. "This is the fabric. See how soft it is? The skirt will go over a light crinoline and have weight in the hem. You'll love the way it dances."

16

If I got my hair wet and braided it tight, I could do it."

"There is no way on earth you are wearing real candles on your head." Carl gave an exaggerated shudder. "I don't mind you serving me breakfast in bed, but you might set my sheets on fire."

"Daddy!" Sarah laughed. "Is that all you care about—setting your sheets on fire? What about me?"

"None of you are wearing real candles. Didn't we just buy a new and expensive battery-operated wreath?"

Constance refilled his coffee cup. "I returned it. It had LED lights, and it made Adrienne look more like a lighthouse than a saint."

"Nothing could make Adrienne look like a saint," Jeffrey said. "It doesn't matter what color light bulbs you use." He caught the orange his sister threw at him and lobbed it back. "Just sayin', Sis. You have a natural devilish glint in your eye."

"Brian's going to see what he can come up with," Constance said.

"We're sure getting our money's worth out of that electrical engineering degree." Jeffrey rose from the table. "Thanks for breakfast. I—"

Penny interrupted. "What's that supposed to mean?"

Jeffrey glanced over his shoulder as he left the room. "Nothing. Just that it's handy to have an electrician around, and he's been hanging around here ever since he got back. A little like a ... lap dog?"

"Jeffrey!"

He grinned at the combined reproaches of his parents. "Sorry. I like him. You should put him out of his misery."

"Jeffrey!" Both parents, more exasperated. He waved and disappeared.

Penny fumed. "Brian isn't miserable. He's a friend. A friend of all of us."

"Don't you like him, Penny?"

"I do, Sadie. I like him a lot, but if people keep talking like he's a boyfriend, he might get scared off and I won't have my friend anymore."

"Brian's not scared of anything," Sarah said. "Angel says he climbed up on the roof to get her kite and then it flew off into a tree and he had to climb the tree from the roof." She used her hands to illustrate the action.

Penny shivered. "I didn't need to know that. I'm not sure that's a sign of bravery, but I'm glad he got Angel's kite for her."

Sarah bit into her orange slice and spoke through the rind. "He didn't. It was too high, so he bought her a new one."

"That's Brian," Penny said. "I bet it was a bigger and better one, too, that would be easier for her to fly and hold onto."

"It had a panda bear on it. Angel loves panda bears."

"Do you really think Brian wouldn't be your friend anymore if people think he's your boyfriend?" Adrienne had obviously put thought into the question, so Penny tried to explain.

"It's awkward. It puts him in an awkward position, and me, too. And then we can't relate naturally, like we used to do."

"Anyhow," Sarah interrupted, "if Brian gets a battery-operated crown, can I be Santa Lucia this year?"

Her father shook his head. "Let Adrienne do it for another year or two. Besides, what will we do when she grows up and you do it? You won't have any attendants."

"You should have had more kids," Sarah said.

"Besides, you need to learn the songs." Adrienne used a knife to peel the orange Jeffrey had thrown back to her. "You only know the first few words and then you hum the rest."

"No, I sing 'la la la' when I don't know all the words."

"You only know the Santa Lucia part!"

"You're lucky. Mom tried to get me to sing it in Swedish," Penny said. "It didn't work out."

Her mother shook her head. "The boys only participated because I bribed them, and there's no way they would have learned a song they couldn't understand."

"It doesn't make a lot of sense in English," Adrienne said. "By the way, I did some research on St. Lucia. I don't know who decided it would be a fun thing for kids to do at Christmas. The story is gruesome."

"Don't dwell on it," Penny advised.

"It's hard not to, when you've got candles on your head," her sister continued, "and the boys' costumes are creepy."

Constance stood up. "I like it, and so do your grandparents. It's part of your heritage."

"Lucia was an Italian Catholic martyr. How is that part of our heritage?"

Constance ignored Adrienne's complaint and began gathering dishes. "There's lots of work to do today. Penny, will you be here for dinner?"

"I should be." She picked up the coffee pot and followed her mother into the kitchen. "Did you talk to Aunt Violet? Dad says she told him she's not ready to talk about the box, and that's exactly what she said to me: 'I'm not ready to talk about it.'"

"Me, too. We'll just have to respect that." Constance leaned against the island and narrowed her eyes at her daughter. "Have you seen that Princess Bride movie?"

Penny blinked. "Yes. I love it. Why?"

"Just wondering." Constance patted her cheek as she passed. "I do love you."

"Hi!" Brittany climbed the steps and stepped inside. "Winter is coming."

"Are you dreaming of a white Christmas?" Penny took the girl's coat. "I've got some ideas for you."

"Yeah, well, we may need to modify things." Brittany dropped onto a chair. "Andy wasn't impressed

The Christmas Glory Quilt

with the movie. He thought it was hilarious, especially the idea of the Santa suits."

"Did you really think he would wear a Santa suit?" Penny asked gently. "I wondered if you were mostly thinking of the ladies' dresses and the flower girls."

"Honestly, I hadn't thought about the men's outfits at all." She shrugged. "It's just those red dresses with the white fur are so gorgeous. I've always loved them. And the muffs. When I was a little girl, I always wanted capes and muffs. I thought they were so elegant."

"They are. I liked them, too."

"Andy said I can wear whatever I want, but he's wearing a black suit."

"Black suits are classic," Penny said, "so if you wanted to go with a White Christmas movie theme, they'd work." She turned her sketchpad around so the girl could see it. "What if you wore a red dress— something simple in shape, but with a flared skirt like that? It would have enough weight to swing around like they do in the movie. And then..." She flipped the page. "You have a coat to go over it for pictures and whenever you're outside."

"Oh." The girl turned the page back and forth, examining the dress and coat. "That might work!"

"I can make a muff," Penny said, "but you might find it a nuisance. You won't want it hanging around your neck on a string, or to hold onto it in one hand. But I can make it if you want. It would be pretty in the pictures."

"What about the bridesmaid? She might be more on board if she has a coat instead of the heavy dress."

Penny turned another page. "I know you like the red, but you know, that scene in the movie wasn't a wedding scene. That's why it worked to have both girls dressed the same. In my opinion, you need to be the star of this show. What if we made the bridesmaid in this black and white fabric? Or this red and white one?" She handed the swatches to Brittany. "When you have the coats on, only the front of the skirt will show, and I think it might look good like that. You still have the red coats and all the white fur. Your outfit will look just like Rosemary Clooney's. Your bridesmaid will have a different skirt fabric, but the shape of the dress will be the same."

She'd made a point of sketching dresses that showed the skirts flaring out, as if they were waltzing. "Because the two of you are in unconventional—unique— gowns, you might consider some kind of headdress. Not a veil, but maybe a crown."

"Oooh." Brittany perked up. "I could do that."

"Something like this. Not a little tiara with jewels, but a crown. You don't have to do that, of course. Just having your hair up would be lovely, and red flowers are authentic to the movie, but a crown would set you off as the bride."

Brittany nodded thoughtfully. "What about my maid of honor?"

Penny pointed to the original picture. "The problem with fur hats—or any hat—is that it makes a mess of your hair. I'd be inclined to not have anything in her hair at all. Is she blonde?"

"Yeah, about the same as me. So, what about the

rest of it? Andy thought it was all ridiculous."

"Well," Penny said, "the boys in the Santa suits would probably be out of place at an elegant wedding."

"I suppose. Can I keep the ballerinas?

"Of course! I like the ballerinas, but I wonder if they'd be more comfortable for the rest of the evening if their costumes—er, dresses looked more like this." She displayed the sketches of full, longer tulle skirts. "You said they'd be in regular ballet slippers, and these would go well. You'd still have them in red and white."

"Their mom did say something about not wanting them in the leotards and tutus for the dinner and reception," Brittany said.

"If you wear a crown, they could have little matching ones, or they could wear wreaths of red and white flowers, if you do that. You might want to think about capes or little jackets for them, for when you're outside."

"I suppose so." Brittany gazed at Penny's drawings. "The men in black suits would look fine with this, wouldn't they?"

"Especially if you go with the black and white fabric for your bridesmaid. Would you like to take these home and show them to your mom and fiancé?"

"Yes, please. Mom's been great about saying she wants me to have whatever I want, but I can tell she's not convinced. I'm not sure I'll show Andy. He's not supposed to see the dress before the wedding, is he? I only showed him the movie because… well, because it's my favorite movie and I wanted to show him my idea."

Penny placed all the sketches and swatches in a

folder and handed it to Brittany. "My fees are in there, so you can look at them and make decisions that you're comfortable with. But I have a proposition for you."

17

I hired someone to do my website and social media stuff."

"Good. It's about time." Faith turned on the windshield wipers. "Isn't this awful weather? You can't do business in the twenty-first century without the internet."

"That's what Liam says. He says word of mouth advertising happens on social media these days."

"That's true," Faith said. "It's where people communicate."

"But don't you think brides are different?"

Faith scoffed. "No! I think brides are online more than anyone else. They say you can't plan a wedding without Pinterest and Instagram. There are whole websites for brides."

"The Knot." Penny nodded. "I think it's mandatory. Brittany is going to take care of all of it. Liam checked her out and he says she knows what she's doing."

"Good." Faith steered the car into the school's parking lot. "If you are going to be in business, do it right."

"It was a kind of turning point. I felt like a real professional business, hiring her. But Liam says I have to tell her about my dyslexia."

"You probably should, if you want her to be helpful." Faith parked the car. "Best spot in the lot."

"Yes, but you have to get here fifteen minutes early to get it! Angel's a bright girl. She could find you if you were two or three cars back. Not to mention that big poufy thing you have on your antenna... it's hard to miss."

Her friend grinned. "So, I get nervous. Sue me."

"Speaking of that, Liam says I should have liability insurance."

"Don't you?"

Penny deflated under Faith's exasperated tone. "I thought I did, but it turns out it's homeowner's liability insurance, and apparently I need something else for the business, in case I stick a bride with a pin or something."

"You keep saying 'Liam says', but it seems to me he's just being practical and you're being flaky. You know all those things, and I bet your dad's already talked to you about the insurance. It's like you don't want to succeed!"

Penny adjusted the vent to blow warm air on her feet. "Brian says I'll probably just get married."

"Stop quoting men. And I bet that's not what Brian said."

Penny felt herself flush. "There was more than that."

"Really." Faith turned to look at her. "Like what?"

"Oh, never mind." She wasn't about to share her confused feelings about Brian with his sister. He'd been so friendly, so casual. But every once in a while, something sparked. He wasn't romantic. He just watched out for her, like a brother. Except that night when they watched the movie. Something had been different that night.

"Well, you don't have to tell me if you don't want to, but Brian cares about you. And he's smart. If he said something, it's worth considering."

"I know. He's a good friend. He's like a brother to me."

"Penny. Really?" The incredulity in Faith's voice caught Penny's full attention.

"It's true. He's always watching out for me, like he did for both of us when we were kids. You remember when he went through that knight-in-shining armor stage and wanted us to be princesses?"

"I think he just liked putting us in the playhouse and telling us to stay there while he went out to kill the dragon," said Brian's sister, "and he always rescued you first." She hesitated. "You know, Mom taught Brian he was supposed to be a protector for his sisters, and for a while, he thought of you as one more sister."

"That's what it felt like to me, too. It was fun."

Faith shook her head. "Not always. He got in a lot of trouble for you."

"For me?" Penny raised her brows. "When?"

Faith sighed. "You remember when you went to prom with Will Harnesse?"

"Yeah! He got sick and abandoned me." She remembered the humiliation of that night vividly. She'd waited for him to come back from the bathroom, and then she'd searched the dark bowling alley. No one had seen him, and it was obvious what they thought: she'd been dumped. She got a ride home with another couple, sitting alone in the back seat in her new dress, dirty after the post-prom bowling party. Will had called a few days later, explaining that he'd gotten sick and had to go home.

"That's not what happened," Faith said. "He wasn't sick. He went outside to have a smoke with some of the other guys from the football team. Brian was working there then, and he happened to be taking out the garbage when he heard them. Apparently, the guys were all talking about their plans for the rest of the night." She glanced at Penny. "Their after-prom activities. With their dates."

"Got it." Penny waited.

"One of them said to Will, 'You know Penny can't even read, right?' And Brian started toward them, ready to defend you, and Will said something about not dating you for your brains and what he had planned didn't include a trip to the library."

"What?" Penny sat up straight, outraged.

"Yeah. So, Brian hit him."

"Hit him!"

"And Will hit him back, but the owner of the bowling alley came out before anything else could happen. He stopped it and threatened to call the police, but the guys backed down. They didn't want to get in trouble. But Brian got fired. I only know about it because Brian had to explain it to Dad, who extracted every detail of the event." Faith finished in a complacent tone. "I hid behind the door and listened."

"Brian got fired because of me? I never heard anything about that."

"Just don't tell Brian I told you. He doesn't even know I know about it. Look—the kids are coming out. But

Brian's not just a good friend. He's always felt more than that."

18

Penny led Liam through the kitchen. "It's really nice of you to bring lunch."

"The Pine Tree's sandwiches are awesome. I wanted one for myself, and I couldn't eat alone. Besides, we won't get many more days like this one. There was frost on my car this morning."

They emerged into the bright sunlight to find Brian sitting at the patio table. His Bible rested on the table next to his lunch box, and he was leaning back with his eyes shut. At their approach, he sat up.

"Do you mind if we join you?" Penny set the cups of soda on the table.

"Sorry to interrupt you." Liam nodded at the Bible. "If you want some privacy, we could sit on the front steps and eat."

"No, that's fine. I'm done." Brian tucked the Bible into his lunch box and pulled out a sandwich. He peeked inside the waxed paper and grinned. "Peanut butter and jelly. My siblings were going on a field trip today, so Mom packed bag lunches for everyone, including me. I also have apple slices, a fruit cup and some carrot sticks."

"Your mom's peanut butter sandwiches are pretty deluxe." She turned to Liam. "Homemade bread with natural peanut butter and homemade strawberry jam."

"What do you have there?" Brian asked.

"I don't know. Liam picked it out, from The Pine Tree."

"That new vegetarian place." Brian looked skeptical. "How do you make a vegetarian sandwich?"

"Well, you could put peanut butter and jelly on it." Penny unwrapped her sandwich. "It looks like a nice multigrain bread."

"Sprouted," Liam corrected. "And it's not all vegetarian. This one is called the Lakelander. It has turkey, lettuce, zucchini, alfalfa sprouts and tomatoes." He took a bite.

"Zucchini?"

Penny laughed at Brian's reaction. "It's just sliced thin. It's doesn't have a lot of flavor of its own." She eyed his sandwich. Liam would probably be offended if she offered to swap sandwich halves with Brian, but it looked delicious.

"I got the sign up," Brian said.

It took Penny a few seconds to realize what he meant. "Oh! I've got to go see it." She covered her sandwich with her napkin. "Did you see it, Liam?"

He shook his head. "I must have missed it. Let's go look." He held out his hand and she let him pull her to her feet.

Brian followed them around the house. "It looks pretty good. Next year you might put some flowers around it or something."

Penny came to a stop at the corner of the house. The simple and elegant sign—just the right size—hung from an iron frame in the front yard.

"Penny Anderson Designs. I like it." Liam walked

forward and circled the sign. It has a nice ring to it. Penny Anderson Designs."

"It won't limit you to wedding dresses, either," Brian commented.

"Wedding dresses are the most profitable," Liam said. "It's a good use of your name. Not too casual or stuffy."

"Stuffy? Remember, you thought Aunt Violet must be Penelope, because it was such an old-fashioned name."

"It's growing on me. It's a sweet name, like some kind of flower. But I like Penny better." Liam smiled down at her.

"I like Penelope."

She knew where this was going. "Brian…"

"I named my goat Penelope."

Liam raised his brows. "You have a goat named Penelope?"

"He named it after me." Penny narrowed her eyes at Brian.

"It was a compliment! I liked that goat."

"You have a goat named after you," Liam beamed at Penny. "That's very flattering."

"No, I don't. It was a meat goat."

Liam burst into laughter. "That's kind of sick."

"She got a second-place ribbon," Brian said. "And sold for a hundred bucks at the 4H auction."

"He always brings up the second-place thing," Penny said to Liam. "My goat took third."

"You don't seem like the goat type," Liam said.

"Oh, yeah. Goats, chickens, dogs and cats. You name it, my mom's raised it and I've cleaned up after it."

"I've never had pets," Liam said. "My mom's allergic."

"That's terrible!"

He shrugged. "Maybe I'll get a dog someday, when I've bought a house and settled down."

An only child without pets. So sad and lonely. Penny led them back to the patio and they resumed their meal.

When Brian finished his sandwich, he rose. "See you guys later."

He walked around the side of the house, and Penny wondered if he was leaving. Had she thanked him for putting up the sign?

"You two have been friends for a long time."

"All my life," Penny said, "or at least as long as I can remember. His sister's my best friend."

"And he's like a brother to you?"

She considered the question. "No, not really like a brother. More like a family member, because I've known him all my life, but not a brother."

He probably thought of himself that way, though. Faith was wrong in her interpretation of the prom fiasco. Brian's defense was exactly what a big brother would have done if a guy talked about his sister like Will talked about Penny.

"How about a cousin?"

"Hm. No, not a cousin. Just a friend who's been there forever. A good friend."

Penny wadded up the sandwich wrapper and napkin. She knew what Liam meant, but it was a stupid question. 'More than a friend' implied the friendship relationship lacked something better. Did it? She wasn't going to hash it over with Liam. He was a nice guy, and she was grateful for his help, but her relationship—her friendship—with Brian was none of his business.

Liam jumped up to help with the garbage. "So, did you listen to that podcast I sent you?"

"Yes. It was complicated. I can't do all that."

"You can automate a lot of it."

"Liam, I don't want to. It's too much."

"Okay." He pushed his hair back. It flopped forward again. "So, we need to figure out which things would be most beneficial."

"No, I have a plan. Come on inside and I'll tell you all about it."

19

This is Buster, right?" Penny wrinkled her nose and rubbed a stick of butter over the turkey's naked back. "I never did like him."

"He was sweet when he was younger." Her mother opened the oven door. "Can you lift that?"

"Just barely." Penny slid the roasting pan into the oven and straightened. "How many people are we expecting?"

"Just us and Nicole's parents. Uncle Gary might come, and if he does, he'll probably bring a date."

"That wasn't gossip!" Penny returned the potholders to the drawer. "Just a comment. All of his dates are nice. He even marries some of them. Ouch!" She flexed her hand. "If you break my fingers, I won't be able to sew, and Penny Anderson Designs will crash before it gets going."

Her mother dropped the wooden spoon in the sink. "Stop that."

"Sorry. Is he bringing Eleanor? She's moved into the cabin, hasn't she?"

"No," Constance said, "she's going home for Thanksgiving. Your Aunt Kathy would have a fit if her only daughter wasn't home for Thanksgiving."

"But she's my favorite cousin, and I haven't seen her in ages," Penny said. "Not that the competition was tough. The rest of them were all boys and enjoyed tormenting us."

"Penny!" Only an eight-year-old girl could squeal like that. Sarah hurled herself against Penny in a dramatic embrace. "I hardly see you at all anymore! It's really boring around here with just Adrienne and Jeffrey. They never want to do anything with me, and I'm stuck doing school alone all day."

"Um…" Her mother raised her brows. "Didn't you just go roller skating with the homeschool group and then spend the night with Angel and then go shopping with Aunt Violet?"

"Yeah, but they aren't Penny. I miss Penny. She's fun, and she's going to teach me to sew."

"I'm sorry I've been so busy." Penny detached Sarah and squatted to face her. "I have so much work to do at the shop right now. Maybe you can come with me one day."

"Don't do it." Adrienne entered the doorway with Lisa on her heels. "She'll put you to work."

"I don't mind working." The little girl stepped aside so Penny could hug her other sisters. "I'll do whatever she says."

"Scrub floors?" Adrienne tousled Sarah's hair. "I had to wash windows."

"You didn't have to," Penny said, "but you were just standing there. You said you wanted to help."

"I was just being polite."

Penny relaxed in the heat of the kitchen, enjoying the familiar laughter and conversation. She needed this.

"Okay, Penny. Start peeling potatoes."

She jumped at her mother's direction, and the older woman smiled.

"You were just standing there."

Penny gazed down the length of the table. The twins, sitting together as always, hotly debated the merits of Harleys and Hondas. Every few minutes, Jeremy scooped up some applesauce and tried to feed it to his daughter. Little Emma was more interested in the Cheerios her other grandma—Nicole's mother—sprinkled on the high chair tray.

They all joked about having absorbed the Wilsons, certain that the couple would rather spend their holidays with a large, happy family instead of staying home alone. The Andersons welcomed them rather than lose Jeremy, Nicole, and the baby. What did the Wilsons think? They always seemed to enjoy themselves, but was it fair to them? Shouldn't they be allowed to have their own celebrations with their only daughter and her family? Their only grandchild?

The family was changing. Lisa's fiancé was missing. Tim was attached to his own family. He'd want to spend holidays with them. What if Mark found a girl at college—one who didn't live in Minnesota? Would he leave them?

Penny tried to swallow the painful lump in her throat. These times were special. Perfect. It was inevitable that the family would be divided. It should be multiplication, but it sure felt more like division. This was why Brian's mom wanted all of her children to marry within their church. She didn't want to lose them.

"Hey." Her father nudged her. "Pass me the potatoes."

Penny handed him the bowl. "I was thinking about how the family is changing."

"Yep, you're all growing up. Flying the coop. Or the nest, or something like that."

"If you mean the chicken coop," Lisa put in, "definitely. I am never going to have chickens of my own. I ruined my new shoes collecting eggs today."

"Why were you collecting eggs in your new shoes?" Her father pushed a forkful of potatoes through a puddle of gravy.

"Sarah had already put on her new dress, before she remembered she hadn't got the eggs."

They all glanced at Sarah, whose ruffles frothed out around her.

"She looks like a cherry on a cupcake."

"Dad! Don't let her hear you say that. She designed that dress herself. I had some red velvet and white tulle left over, so…" Penny shrugged. "Pretty soon, she'll be too old for ruffles, and we'll miss that."

"Too old for ruffles?" Carl said in mock horror. "Impossible. I've always had girls in ruffles."

"Well, now you have Emma, and probably more to come."

"It's not the same," he grumbled, "but it will have to do." He cast a fatuous glance at his granddaughter, who had smeared sweet potato into her blond curls. "So, is Brian still hanging around the house?"

Penny blinked at the abrupt change in topic. "Hanging around? He doesn't hang around. He's always fixing something or digging in the garden or finding better ways for me to do things."

"I got a call from Hank the other day. He sent one of his guys over to install the outside lights, and they were already done. I assume you didn't do it." Carl shoveled the forkful of potatoes into his mouth.

"I'm starting to feel guilty every time I see him with a toolbox," Penny said. "Not that I don't appreciate it, but I'm beginning to wish you'd never sent him over to help me."

Her father put up a hand. "I just asked him to fix the exit sign. Anything else he's done is on his own, for you."

His truck was already there, on the Friday after Thanksgiving, when most people were sleeping in or shopping. Penny had a cowardly urge to keep driving, but they'd be putting up the Christmas tree tomorrow. Sunday would be busy, too, and she had to work on her dress. Dani's dress. She parked the car.

The steps were icy. She'd have to ask Brian what could be done to make them safe. Penny stopped mid-step. She'd ask her father or call the hardware store. She'd never meant to take advantage of Brian, but that was exactly what she'd done, as if he was an employee. A stranger she'd hired to do a job. A serf.

"Oh, Lord, help me with this." She whispered the

prayer as she was punching in the security code and had to start over. Penny leaned her head against the door. Four digits, and she still messed it up. Brian probably thought she needed a keeper.

The house was quiet. She wandered through the main floor without her usual sense of pleasure, searching but not calling for him. No Brian. Penny hadn't seen evidence of his work in her apartment, but maybe he was moving on to that now that the downstairs was complete.

"Brian? Are you up there?" She flipped on the light and climbed the stairs. The apartment was dark and empty in the November morning, but a thrill ran through her as she touched the wall. This was hers. Her first home of her own. Penny mentally painted and furnished the apartment as she walked through it. She wanted light colors, but not the robin's egg blue she'd used downstairs. Something warm.

She paused in the guest room. The vista was better than her own, overlooking the distant trees that had grown too big, blocking their view of the river, but she'd come for the closer view. Brian slept on the lounge chair she'd set out for Aunt Violet, feet braced on the end of the chair and arms crossed—probably for warmth. The book splayed on the table beside him had to be a Bible. As she watched, he reached out and picked it up, looked at it, and laid it down again.

Penny stepped back, as if he might look up and catch her staring. He was always there, fixing her problems, even anticipating her needs before she felt them, and she offered him casual thanks. Selfish. Self-centered. Careless of her friends. Deeply ashamed, Penny descended the stairs and left the house.

The car was already cold, and she thought of Brian as she turned the key. He must be freezing. She turned the key off and pulled it out, hitting the button to open the trunk. The heavy denim quilt smelled faintly of gasoline, but it would be warm.

The front door opened as she climbed the stairs.

"I thought I heard someone out here!" Brian's gaze moved from her face to the quilt.

Penny lifted it. "I saw you outside."

"Thanks." He took the blanket. "I was ready to come in, but thank you."

He smiled at her, just as if she was a good friend and nice person. Penny wilted.

"Brian, you've done way too much for me. I feel like I'm taking advantage of you." The words tumbled out. "I've been so focused on getting my business started. You've done everything, and I don't even say thank you."

"You say thank you all the time."

"But I don't mean it!" Penny clapped a hand over her mouth and hysterical laughter overrode the wail. "I mean, I do mean it. I am grateful, more than I can say. But…"

Brian cut her off. "Come inside. It's cold out." He continued heaping coals of fire on her head. "I hope you don't mind me being here. I should have asked. Mom was having some kind of craft party, and a teenage girl was babysitting about a hundred kids in the basement. I didn't want to hang out in my bedroom all day, and I don't have the furnace installed at my own house yet. I was desperate."

Penny couldn't help smiling. "So, you came here to hide." She dropped her coat over the chair and walked into the consultation area. "You're welcome to stay as long as you like, of course. I've got some work to do. But Brian, I mean it. You've done so much for me, and you could probably have that furnace in by now if you weren't always busy here."

"No, it hasn't even been delivered yet. I've been waiting on the HVAC guys. And the plumber has to redo some things that didn't pass inspection. Are you working on your Santa Claus wedding today?"

"That one's not until next year. I'm working on Dani Lorris's gown now. Her wedding is New Year's Eve. But what are you doing? Not working, I hope."

He rubbed the back of his neck. "I brought my laptop and thought I'd watch some of those work videos. If you don't mind."

"No, of course not." Penny walked into the workroom and pulled Dani's folder from the cabinet. "It's still work-related, but it's better than doing slave labor for me."

"Not slave labor," Brian said. "I like it."

Penny turned to face him, resolute. "When I found you here—"

"When you broke my nose?"

She ignored the interruption. "You said my dad asked you to put in the exit light and redo some wiring. I thought… well, you said you were between jobs—or at least, that's how I interpreted it. I thought he was paying you to work here."

Brian's smile vanished, and a crease appeared

between his brows. "Paying me?"

"Dad took care of the building stuff. He arranged for contractors and paid the bills."

"Why would you think I'd want to be paid for helping you?"

Penny cringed at his rough tone. "I thought you needed the work. I'm sorry."

"You should be sorry for thinking you had to pay me to help you."

He was right. She should have known. He'd always helped her, followed her around, even defended her honor when Will Harnesse was boasting to his friends. Even if he'd been unemployed, Brian would never have taken money for helping her.

"I'm sorry. You're right. I should have known. I've been so selfish lately, not thinking about anything except getting the shop open—not even you or my family."

"It's your hyper-focused mode."

Was his voice a little softer? Penny searched his face—the same gray eyes, overgrown hair and scruffy beard. Maybe a bump on his nose. She winced.

"Brian, please forgive me. But I do feel guilty for ordering you around like you were getting paid and for thinking you were being paid and had to be paid."

"You were kind of bossy." His tone was definitely lighter. "Is that how you plan to treat your employees when you get some?"

"No! And I shouldn't have ever treated you that way."

He held up a hand. "Please don't say you're sorry again. It's fine. I've been here because I wanted to be."

Was that past tense? Penny opened her mouth, but he continued.

"It never occurred to me that you thought of me as an employee. Could we just drop this?"

How could they? What was she supposed to do now? She'd never be able to ask him for anything, knowing it was a favor he was doing her. A gift.

"Yeah." She managed to get the word out. More needed to be said, but she needed to think. To compose herself. She'd hurt Brian.

20

Violet

So, there were some other *brudkrona* in America. Violet closed the laptop and regarded the small crown. She had silver polish and a cloth, but silver or an alloy wouldn't be flexible, like gold, and if she broke any of the delicate spears and piercing she would never forgive herself.

She picked it up and weighed it on her palm. Had her mother actually worn it? They didn't have a photograph of the wedding. How had it ended up in a box in the garden? Had her father buried it there after his wife died? Grief made people do strange things.

Papa wasn't always grieving, though. He'd been kind and cheerful sometimes. A few times, he told her she looked like her mother. With three marriageable daughters, it would have been natural to mention the *brudkrona*.

Violet picked up her silver cloth and dabbed at the tarnish, but she couldn't bring herself to rub it. Giving up, she rewrapped the little crown and replaced it in the box. Where could she put it out of sight? She wasn't ready to talk about it or show it to the family. She needed time to think. To process, as Penny would say.

Maybe she should call Bonnie and ask if her mother had ever mentioned a bridal crown. Linnea's wedding had been a little hasty, for the usual reason, and according to the rules of the church, that would have made her ineligible to wear the crown anyhow. But there was never any talk of it at the time. Violet would have remembered such a treasure. Maybe Kristina had hidden it, from spite or outraged virtue, but Papa would have mentioned it, wouldn't he?

She resisted the urge to hit the box. It felt like a secret that had unjustly been kept from her. A piece of the mother she should have known: a girl with sunlight hair and sky-blue eyes who laughed and loved her best friend.

She'd take it to a jeweler or museum and get it cleaned up. She wanted to see it as it was when Johannes gave it to his Hilma. The girl he called his light.

21

L iam shifted from one foot to the other, his hand on the doorknob behind him. "Are you absolutely sure you don't want me to wait for you? Or I could come back. I don't want to leave you here without a car."

"It's okay," Dani said. "It's probably best if my new mother-in-law sees that Penny isn't just some farmer's wife who makes dresses. I shouldn't have told her where the shop is. She drove by to see it, and the sign wasn't up yet." She rolled her eyes. "She's been worried about it all week, so I suggested she meet me here."

"She drove by here?" Liam frowned. "Doesn't she trust you to choose your own dress?"

"It's complicated." Dani laughed at her own cliché. "She likes things to be done right. I thought I'd convinced her that using a small-town Minnesota dressmaker would appeal to the voters, but she's not letting go of it."

"She should trust you. You're smart, and you have good taste."

Liam reached out a hand, and Penny decided it was time to remind them of her presence.

"Bye, Liam. I'll think about your suggestions. You're probably right."

He grinned. "I like being right. Bye, Dani. Talk to you later."

The girl gave him a cute wave, and he waved back. Penny pushed him out the door.

"Ready? We should get started. I want to fit the bodice today and measure for the skirt. You brought your shoes and undergarments?"

Dani held up the bag. "I found pretty shoes with two-inch heels. I can dance all night."

"Wear them around the house for a while. You don't want to find out on your wedding day that the straps give you blisters." Penny realized she was snapping and tried to let go of her irritation. Liam had no business charming this girl. She was engaged to someone else. As for Dani... Penny hadn't expected her to be so flighty. "You can change in here. Do you need any help with the undergarments?"

"No. I refuse to wear underwear I can't manage on my own. Just the bra and leggings, right?" Dani kept talking as she walked behind the screen. "I'll have to bring my mom next time. She went shopping with me for the undergarments, and she kept pushing me toward the girdles."

"Girdles?" Penny hadn't heard that word in a while.

"Yeah, like my great grandma used to wear. Mom seems to think I should have something with compression."

"You'll look beautiful." Penny offered the reassuring phrase mechanically, "and you'll be comfortable."

"That's what I want." Dani emerged from behind the screen. "You want me on the box?"

"Yes, please." Penny lifted the muslin and slid it over Dani's arms.

"It's inside out."

"That's how it works," Penny said. She pinched the side seam. "The zipper will go here. Keep your arms up so I don't stab you with a pin. I'll use a pen to draw alterations. The front is good, but I'm going to take it in just a bit at the back waist."

Dani twisted, trying to see what Penny was doing. "I don't know how you can tell, at this point. Is this going to be part of the finished dress?"

"Hold still. This is just a pattern. It's called a muslin, because that's what they're usually made of. I think it fits pretty well." She stepped back and walked around the bride. "What do you think?"

"I'm having trouble imagining it like this," Dani said. "It doesn't look like the picture."

Penny retrieved Dani's folder and pulled out the sketch. "See? You have the basis for the bodice here, with the two seams here." She pointed. "Those are the princess seams that will match up with the ones in the skirt, but you won't see them in the final bodice. The back is smooth because the zipper is under the arm. That won't show, either. And there'll be a soft drape here."

Dani tried to see over her shoulder and squeaked when she encountered a pin. "Okay, I trust you, Penny."

"Ready for your hoop skirt?" Penny laughed at Dani's horrified expression. "Just kidding. It's a crinoline slip. It's lightweight with a narrow waistband. It sits below your natural waist, so it won't roll up when you bend over or cut into your waist when you're eating."

"But it stays up, right? I don't want to show up in one of those funny bride videos, with my slip falling off on the dance floor."

"You're safe. Sometimes the crinoline is built into the gown, but that makes the dress heavier and pulls on the bodice, so the bodice has to be made heavier—more sturdy—and you don't want that. I also find the skirt doesn't swing as well that way." Penny demonstrated, and Dani nodded.

"I definitely want it to swing."

"So, we use a separate slip. Put this one on for now."

Penny relaxed into her most comfortable state, explaining what she was doing and how it would all work together to make Dani feel good and look beautiful. This was her favorite part of the process, when the bride began to see her gown come to life.

"The skirt will be two inches off the floor. That's a good length for walking and dancing, but if you plan to take your shoes off at all, the skirt will touch the floor."

A frown creased Dani's brow. "I thought it would be floor-length."

"It will look and feel floor-length, but you don't want it to actually touch the floor or it won't swing freely. Let me get some pictures."

When Dani returned to the changing room twenty minutes later, smiling, Penny laid aside the skirt pieces and picked up the muslin bodice. She held it to her chest and turned slightly in front of the mirror. Unlike Dani, she could visualize it perfectly.

A series of chimes sounded in the changing room,

and Dani came out, tapping her phone.

"Catherine will be here in about five minutes."

"Should we leave things out, so she can see them?"

"No, let's put everything away. If she sees it now, she'll start picking it apart." Dani shoved the phone into her bag. "She cares a lot about what other people think, and she doesn't seem to understand that most people don't think about other people at all. Except her. She's always thinking about other people in a negative way."

"Ugh. I hope your fiancé is better than his mother."

"Oh, yes. John's fine."

"Fine?" The question came out before Penny could stop it.

Dani flushed. "He's wonderful. Very romantic and thoughtful. Nice manners. He does care what people think, though, because he's in politics. He's been an aide to Senator Denkins for years, and he was going to start by running for school board, but his mother's the principal at a private school in St. Cloud, so there was a conflict of interest. So, he changed his mind at the last minute, and now he's running for district assembly."

"John." Stunned, Penny groped for the workbench stool and sat. "Is your fiancé John Trandle?"

"Yes! Do you know him?" Dani beamed. "I suppose you went to school with him at SCSU. That's where we met, at a fundraiser for the new library."

It was a horrible, unbelievable coincidence, and there was no way she could stand and make pleasant conversation with Catherine Trandle. She couldn't do it.

"You know, I'm really not feeling well."

"You do look pale, but you were fine a minute

ago." Dani sat down on the other stool and stared at Penny.

"Not anymore," Penny muttered. She stood up. "Your future mother-in-law and I did not get along. She won't want me making your wedding dress."

"Why not?"

Dani didn't stand up, so Penny sat down again. She couldn't tell Dani that the woman was afraid of having grandchildren who couldn't read or write. That John's dad couldn't decide whether her disability would be a political asset or a social handicap. That John had regretfully ended their relationship because they were incompatible. He wished her well.

Before she could compose a response, the doorbell rang. Penny closed her eyes and sent up a silent, desperate prayer.

"Well, Penny! How nice to see you again!" Catherine Trandle had social skills.

Penny didn't. She smiled and nodded.

"Penny was just telling me that she knew you," Dani said. "Didn't I tell you her name when we talked about the dress? I guess I never called John by his last name, either."

Catherine ignored her, looking around with interest. "This is a lovely place, Penny. I'm so glad you found a suitable career for yourself. I remember John said you made your own clothes. Are you doing well here?"

Penny refused to let the woman crush her as she had four years ago. "Yes, I am, thank you. I hope you are well."

Dani looked from Catherine to Penny and back

again. "It's more than a suitable career, Catherine. She's a top-quality bridal gown designer. You should see her portfolio."

"Wonderful." The older woman smiled with all her teeth. "I'm so happy for you. And how are all your family? Still homeschooling?"

"Oh, yes." Penny displayed her own teeth. "The younger ones are still homeschooled. Jeremy just finished his respiratory therapist degree, and Mark's getting ready to start med school. Lisa's in the second year of her RN program. Everyone seems to be doing just fine academically." She reined in her compensatory snark. "Thank you for asking."

Dani looked alarmed. Penny gave her a sympathetic smile. Poor girl. She was too sweet to be married into the Trandle family.

22

H i."

She couldn't see him in the dusk, but she wasn't surprised. Brian was always there.

"I'm going to be gone for a while. Just wanted to let you know."

Penny sat up and swung her legs over the side of the lounge chair. "Where are you going?" Ugh. She didn't have any right to ask that—at least, not in that demanding tone. She tried again. "You startled me."

He came out of the shadows, and she could see him in the thin light of the moon. "I need to get some work done on my house before the weather turns bad."

"You've been spending all your time here, on my house," Penny said. "I don't know what I would have done without you."

"You would've figured it out."

"It wouldn't be as good. You made all those details perfect." She prayed he couldn't see her face. It was probably a splotchy mess before he arrived, and he was making it worse. No, it wasn't his fault. He'd done nothing but good for her.

"I enjoyed it. It was interesting to see your creative world."

"My creative world? That makes it sound so artistic and elegant."

"Well, you are artistic, and if not elegant… you have style."

A rush of pleasure eased the pain in her chest.

"Thank you. I'm so grateful."

"Stop saying that." He moved closer and squatted down next to her. "It's dark out here. Have you been crying?"

She sniffled. She hadn't meant to. Brian put his arms around her. It was an awkward embrace. He rose and sat next to her on the chair. She leaned against him, and he put an arm around her shoulders.

"Tell me about it."

She sobbed. If he'd asked her what was wrong, she would have said 'nothing' or attempted a casual response. Instead, he invited her to share her problems. That was Brian.

She told him everything. Every so often, he squeezed her shoulder and pulled her closer to him, and he made a few sympathetic sounds, but he didn't say anything. Once she finished with the Trandles, she embarked on the story of the wedding dress, and she finished up with her failures as a businesswoman.

When it was over, they sat in silence, in the dark, watching clouds slide over the moon. Winter breezes brushed their faces.

"Can I have a corner of this thing?" Brian plucked at the edge of the quilt. "It's cold out here."

Penny rearranged the quilt to drape over their shoulders. "This is warm. It weighs a ton, and it's not even finished."

"One of your aunt's projects?"

"She says this one is for my parents. I hope they don't plan to leave it to me someday. Violet calls them family history quilts. This one has blocks for my parents, their parents and grandparents, each of us kids and our kids. That's why it's not done."

Brian lifted his end of the quilt and peered at it. He dug in his pocket, pulled out his phone and used the flashlight to see it better.

"I had a tie just like this one. I remember, because it's really ugly. Mom made it to match my sisters' dresses one Easter. I was about twelve. It was traumatic."

"Maybe the fabric came from Faith's dress. She was—is—my best friend, and she was always hanging around the house. See—this one was my prom dress." She hastened on, not wanting to talk about prom. "And this Little Pony fabric had to be me. I had at least a hundred little ponies. Here's a heart cut from my bridesmaid dress from Faith's wedding."

"But that strip is shaped like a tie, and it looks like it's going through that heart shape." He moved the flashlight over the block. "Look. That's the jersey I wore for basketball."

"Well, you were my friend, too. What is that on the tie?"

Brian lifted it and held the flashlight closer.

Penny heard him inhale. "What does it say?"

"Sorry. Um… it looks like she wrote on it. It says, 'Penelope and Brian'."

Penny snatched it from him. The letters were too small and close together, especially in the dark. "It does not!"

He let out a breath of laughter. "It does. Want me to find a magnifying glass?"

"That is really weird. Why would she do that?"

Brian shifted. "Well, maybe she thought... I don't know. Those are old pieces of fabric. She couldn't have known..."

"Known what?" Penny felt herself breathing faster. "Why would she do that?"

"Apparently she thought we'd... end up together. Get married."

"That long ago?" Penny examined the block again. "I mean, even if she made it recently, what would have made her think we'd get married?"

"I don't think she made it recently. Faith's wedding was ten years ago, and why would she hang onto my clothes? It's kind of creepy."

"Really creepy," Penny said. "And ridiculous."

"Ridiculous?" Brian's tone was even.

"Well, we were just kids. And now, we're friends. Good friends."

"Penny." His voice was tender.

She jumped to her feet, disentangling herself from the quilt and leaving it on the chair next to Brian. She wouldn't run away, but she walked fast.

"Penny!"

She yanked open the door and tripped over the threshold. Brian was there before she could fall.

"You'll break your neck in the dark. Why didn't you turn the light on?"

"You need to go build your house, Brian."

"I'll be back in a few days." He grasped her

shoulders and turned her to face him. "Maybe your aunt is a wise woman. She understands people, like you do. But you don't seem to understand how I feel, Penny, or even see me at all."

His hands slid around her back and he drew her against him. She could feel his ragged breath on her hair.

"Brian, I..."

He stepped back and ran his fingers along the side of her face. "Just... try to see me, Penny. Don't be so blind, so focused on outward things. I'm not just your friend."

His kiss was gentle, but it demanded a response. Penny lifted her hands and rested them on his strong arms. She leaned in, closing her eyes and trying to see him. His hands moved to the back of her head, cradling it, not pressuring her but holding her gently.

Penny didn't see Brian when she closed her eyes. She saw her life without Brian. And it was sad. Brian was a part of her. But he wasn't just a part of her. Not an appendage. She stepped back, and he let her go, but he slid his hands down to hold hers.

"Your hands are cold. Let's get inside."

She realized the door was still open. He ran back to grab the quilt—the troublesome quilt—and pushed her inside the house, closing the door behind him.

"Do you want to talk, Penny?"

Did she? She shook her head. "I need to think."

Brian watched her, his brows drawn together. "Okay, think. But think about this. I am your friend. And I'll try to go on being your friend, but things just changed. Not in me. I've felt this way for years. Forever. But between us. And I think it's time. Past time." He looked around. "Are you staying here or going home?"

"Home."

"I'll follow you."

That was it. That was Brian. Penny thought suddenly of a movie she'd watched with her sisters. The one Mom mentioned a few weeks ago. In The Princess Bride, the hero said 'as you wish', and it meant 'I love you.'

"Thanks." She couldn't think of anything else to say. If she said the wrong things, in a hurry without thinking, something bad might happen.

Outside, he paused. "Penny, ask your dad about the conversation we had a while ago. Tell him I said it was okay."

23

Carl leaned back against the booth and took a sip of his coffee.

"He told me to ask you what happened at your last conversation." Penny examined his frowning face. Dad didn't frown often. "He said to tell you it was okay."

He heaved a sigh. "It was a long time ago."

"It can't have been that long ago. He's only been back for a couple months."

"No, I think he's talking about a conversation we had nearly ten years ago." He counted on his fingers. "Eight. You were seventeen."

"You've talked to him since then. Why would he be talking about something you said eight years ago?"

"Well…" Another sip of the coffee. "Brian wanted to come talk to me. He set up an appointment. I thought maybe he wanted a job, but he came with his parents—both of them—and he asked me for permission to court you."

"What?" Penny's hand jerked, nearly spilling her juice.

"He had it all mapped out on paper. It was a list of courtship rules and plans for activities that included either all four of us parents or your brothers and sisters. He wanted to do a Bible study with me, so I could know his intentions were honorable and he'd make a good husband and support you. His mother just sat there nodding and smiling." Carl snorted. "A list of rules for courtship!"

"What did you say?"

"I said no, of course!"

She couldn't help laughing at his indignant response. "Why didn't you tell me?"

"Because Brian was a nice boy." Her dad set his cup on the table. "He still is, and he's grown up a lot. I think the two of you would be a good match."

"Now, but not then?"

"No. I wasn't going to subject you to Denise Michaels and her rules for Christian ladies. They wanted you to go to church with them, too, and that wasn't gonna happen. Besides, Brian needed to grow up. He was 18— too old to be taking his mother along for something like that."

"You should have told me."

"Brian asked me not to. He came to the site the next day, where I was working, and he asked me to not tell you about the meeting. He said he was going away to college, and when he came back, if you were still single, he'd try again."

Her dad poured syrup over his stack of pancakes. "I gave him my blessing for that."

"You did? And you still didn't tell me."

"I just said he didn't want me to. I respected that. He was embarrassed, and he's been a good friend to you. He still is." He chewed a mouthful of pancake.

"But he was gone a lot longer than just four years for college."

Her dad shrugged. "He got a job. Then you were at college and dating that stuffed-shirt guy."

"You never told me you didn't like him!"

"Nothin' to like. He'll probably go far in the world, but he's as much a mama's boy as Brian was."

"But Brian's not anymore." Penny remembered their conversation. "He respects her. He says she lives by her convictions."

"Yeah, but she thinks the rest of us should live by her convictions, too."

"He said she's judgmental, but she does it because she really believes that we're wrong and need to be saved."

"We are saved. And for us, it's grace that saves us, not her list of rules and regulations. Not works."

"I'm not explaining it well. The thing is, if she really believes we're wrong and not saved, shouldn't she try to tell us?"

Her dad shook his head. "That doesn't make sense."

"It does, the way he explains it, but he doesn't agree with her. That's why he goes to Riverdale now."

"Respecting her is a good thing," Carl said, "as long as he doesn't expect you to be like her."

"No, he doesn't. But I don't know what to do!"

"'Bout what?" Carl continued to eat, running a forkful of pancake through a puddle of syrup and melted butter.

"About Brian!"

"Why? Did he ask you to marry him?" Her dad sat up with a pleased smile. "It's about time."

"Dad! No, he didn't ask me. But…" Penny ran her finger around the edge of her glass. "Things changed. He, uh, kissed me."

"Really! Well, that's a good start. Did you kiss him back?"

Penny chuckled. "Sort of. It was all so sudden. And you know what started it?" She corrected herself. "At least, it sort of brought it to a head. Aunt Violet's old quilt. The one she's making for you and Mom."

"What about it?"

"Do you know what she does?" Penny asked.

"Yeah, she's been making those forever. She writes books to go with them. Did you know that?"

"She told me that just recently," Penny admitted. "I hadn't paid much attention to her quilts. I've always thought they were pretty ugly."

"Yeah, well, they are, but once you understand them, they're pretty interesting. She's got parts about everyone in the family, and they're explained in the books. Your mom says it's like a scrapbook. They all start with her grandparents, who immigrated and set up the farm. Then her parents and siblings. From what I understand, she's separated them out after that, so our quilt doesn't include your cousins and distant relatives." He took a long drink of orange juice.

"Well, apparently she's not quite done with yours," Penny said, "because you still have unmarried kids and only one grandchild. The thing is, she's already married me off. To Brian."

Her father set down his glass. "You're kidding."

"There's a block in that quilt with fabrics from our

old clothes, and she's written 'Penelope and Brian' on it. Even a heart shape. It seems pretty obvious."

"Is it new? You have been hanging around together." Carl grinned. "Just about every day, from what I hear."

"How could it be new? She's got patches from when Brian was twelve years old!"

"She's a smart woman, Penny. If she says you should marry him, you should give it some thought." Her dad stood, pulled out his wallet and threw a twenty-dollar bill on the table. "I like Brian."

24

P enny!" Dani ran from her car and gave Penny a hug. "I wanted to call you and talk, but then I chickened out and just waited. I'm so sorry for what Catherine said. She's just vile. When I asked John about it, he got defensive. He said you broke up with him."

That wasn't how Penny remembered it. "We weren't well-suited. I'm not a political wife. We parted on good terms, and neither of us have any regrets. The two of you are perfect together." She'd practiced that in front of the mirror before Dani arrived, and it came out smoothly.

Dani talked as they entered the house and hung up their coats. "I think you made him realize that his wife had to want the same things he did. He told me about his political ambitions when we started dating, and we talked about it a lot later, before we got engaged."

"We weren't that serious, Dani." She'd thought they were, though, before his parents found out about her dyslexia. Dani and John had similar careers, interests, social circles and families, and Dani was prepared for the demands John's political career would place on her. She seemed comfortable in that world.

"I brought the pictures from the hair stylist." Dani lifted a strand of hair. "She managed to turn this bob into an updo. It looks pretty good. Mom's thrilled I'm going to wear her diamond clip. I think it's the first time I've made her happy since the dress burned down."

"Did you bring it with you?" Penny asked.

"It's in my bag. It's smaller than I remembered. I'd call it a comb. The stylist said I could wear it here and hang a veil from it." Dani pushed her hands up under her hair. "Or she can put it on the side if I don't want a veil. I told her you said I have to try on the dress before I decide."

Penny led her into the fitting room. "You'll be able to try it on today. I have a few details left, but the dress is mostly finished." She smiled. "You'll be a lot happier to see the bodice put together right side out."

Dani disappeared behind the screen. "I've never been good at visualizing things like that. I can't look at a blue dress and think what it would look like in red."

Penny paused. She could see that inside-out muslin in every color of the rainbow, prints, plaids and stripes. In her mind, as well as in reality, she could determine the necessary alterations, cut it apart, turn it right side-out, add sleeves, change the neckline and sew it all together. She was good at that kind of vision. It was a gift.

Catherine Trandle and people like her only saw her inability to read well and wrapped their entire opinion of her around that detail. Their vision of her stopped at her dyslexia. It was hard to not be frustrated—or hurt—by that.

"Okay, I'm ready!" Dani came out of the changing room and stepped into the crinoline slip.

"Stand on the box," Penny said. She pulled the

curtain over the mirror. This was the big moment, and it deserved her full attention.

Dani hopped onto the box and shivered in excitement as Penny gathered the dress and dropped it over her head. The fabric fell into place, and Penny zipped it closed. She tweaked folds and gently tugged on the skirt, making sure that when Dani saw her reflection, it would be perfect. The gown of her dreams. The gown of Penny's dreams.

With a dramatic flourish, Penny pulled the cord and the curtains swept aside. She liked to watch the bride's face at this moment rather than the dress. Dani didn't disappoint her. The big brown eyes opened in astonishment. Her lips parted, but she didn't speak. She twisted to see reflections in the side mirrors.

"I love it."

Penny smiled at the girl's wonder. This was the joy in what she did—making dreams come true. Making women feel beautiful and happy, and accomplishing it with the gifts and skills God had given her. She needed to store up this memory, to pull out when she felt inadequate or irritated with the process.

"Can I get down?"

"Yes, of course." Penny held Dani's hand as she descended from the box. "Come over here, where there's more room."

Dani twirled like a three-year-old and then waltzed. The skirt behaved just as it ought, turning from the waist and then the hem catching up, swaying freely. Dani threw her arms around Penny. "I love it. It's perfect, and you're a genius. Thank you, thank you, thank you!"

She let Dani preen and sway in front of the mirrors for a few more minutes. The dress was everything she'd imagined it would be, and it was rewarding to see this bride's delight in it.

"If you stand on the box again, I'll measure for the veil, and then you can change clothes."

Dani held the skirt in both hands as she stepped up. "I don't want to take it off."

"Just a couple more weeks," Penny said. "We'll do one more quick fitting next week, with the veil, and then you'll be ready for the wedding!"

Dani sat on the stool, watching her reflection. "This is great. Just what I needed." She lifted her hair. "The stylist thought it should go right about here."

"Okay." Penny fastened the accessory to Dani's hair and grabbed a length of tulle from the table.

"I don't quite get the point of veils," Dani commented. "Not this kind of veil, anyhow."

"It's pretty, and it will make you feel pretty."

"I do. I needed this today."

Penny took the pins from her mouth. "What do you mean?"

"It's been a long week. I think I'm going through the cold feet stage. Like the nesting stage pregnant women go through."

"Um... I don't think there's supposed to be a cold feet stage." The words came out before she thought about them. She stuffed the pins back in, hoping to stop any further slippage.

"Really? Well, it's bridal jitters, then. I've heard of that one."

Penny continued to pin the tulle into pleats, hoping she didn't poke her tongue. Whatever her own opinion of John Trandle, this was Dani's life, and Penny had to keep her mouth shut. If she opened it, the pins would fall out.

"I know there's this leaving and cleaving thing," Dani said, "but even if a man does that, he doesn't—shouldn't—divorce his family. They always say that the best way to judge a potential husband is by the way he treats his mother. When it comes right down to it, a man and his mother come as a package deal."

Penny thought about Brian and his mother. He disagreed with her on some major issues, but she'd never heard him be anything but respectful and affectionate. Denise Michaels and Catherine Trandle had different objectives in life, but they both saw and judged people by their outward appearance and conformity to certain standards. Unlike John, Brian didn't let his mother manage him.

As if reading her mind, Dani asked, "Are you dating that blond guy I see around here all the time?"

"No, he's an old friend. I couldn't have done all of this without him. It was a bigger project than I'd anticipated." Penny caught Dani's eyes in the mirror. "I'd be in trouble without him."

"Just an old friend? He sure seems to be here a lot for an old friend."

He did. In the last few days, Brian had gone back to being an old friend, with no talk of changing relationships and how he felt about her. Their kiss might never have happened. There was no mention of Aunt Violet's quilt or—

"And he's cute."

Cute? Brian was good-looking, in a rugged kind of outdoorsy, unshaven way. She'd have to tell him Dani thought he was cute.

"What do you think?" Penny secured the clip and veil at the back of Dani's head. "Veil or no veil? It's just tacked in place to give you a visual. The real one will look better than that."

The girl walked over to the mirrors and turned, looking over her shoulders. "I don't know. What do you think?"

Penny hadn't considered a veil; she'd been more into tiaras at twelve years old. "I think it's fine either way. You can always remove the veil after the wedding if you like. It just hooks onto the clip."

"Let's do it." Dani returned so Penny could remove the accessories. "When do you want me to come back?"

Penny consulted her list. "A week from Friday? That's the 14th."

Dani shook her head. "I'll be out of town. How about Thursday?"

"That's Santa Lucia Day. It's a holiday for my family."

"Is that the girl with the candles?" Dani looked at Penny's blond ponytail. "Do you dress up like that?"

"Not anymore. I passed the torch—candles—to my sister, Lisa, a few years ago, and now another sister is doing it. The candles aren't real, though. Could you come on Wednesday morning?"

Dani consulted her phone. "That works for me. Nine o'clock?"

"Yes. Bring everything you'll be wearing, including your shoes, and have your hair done."

"Great!" Dani headed for the door and stopped abruptly to avoid running into Brian. "Hey there."

"Sorry." Brian moved aside to let her pass. "I'm always in the way."

Dani dimpled at him. "Penny said she'd be in trouble without your help, so I think you're excused."

She waved at Penny. "See you next week!"

25

T hanks, Liam. I really appreciate your help."
Penny grasped the box, but Liam didn't release it.
"I'll carry it. Fabric is heavier than you'd think."

"Believe me... I know how heavy it is. I should be built like a power lifter by now."

Liam waggled his dark brows as he set the box on the table. "I like you better the way you are."

"Is that a man bun?"

Brian's voice was unnecessarily loud. And rude. Penny rolled her eyes.

Liam grinned. "Yeah. What do you think?" He tipped his head to one side and regarded Brian's shaggy head. "I don't think you have enough to do it yet. Keep trying." He turned to wave at Penny on his way out. "I'll see you next week."

Penny laughed at the expression on Brian's face. "Gotcha."

Brian ran a hand through his hair. "I guess it's not much shorter than his. I just don't have those pretty brown ringlets."

"Are you jealous of Liam's hair?"

"No, I just don't have enough hair product to achieve that look."

"Brian! Shame on you." Penny removed bolts of fabric from the box and laid them on the cutting table.

"I need a haircut. It ends up long because I never think to get it cut when the barber shop's open."

"You could get your mom to cut it."

Brian shook his head. "She only has one style, and I'm too old for that look."

"But you were such a cute little boy!"

"Especially on Sunday in my suit and tie. I looked exactly like all the other little boys in my church, right down to the right-side part in my hair."

"I know! I asked my mom if we could go to your church because the girls all got to wear nice dresses and you boys were so handsome and well-behaved." Penny tossed the empty box toward the door. "She said no."

"I'm still handsome and well-behaved." Brian walked over and picked up the box. "And helpful. I'll carry this heavy box out to the garage for you."

"I've never seen one of these in real life." Penny touched the head of the quilting machine as if it might bite. "You know how to use this?"

"I've been renting it at the quilt shop in Princeton for years. They let you pay by the hour and teach you how to use it." Violet looked with satisfaction at the long-arm quilter. "I've never had room for one before, until now. When they closed last month, I bought it. The owner's husband came out and set it up for me."

"It looks kind of scary. How does it work?" Penny squatted to examine the roller bars. Are we really going to get this quilt done today?"

"Not done, but if we get it loaded, I can do the rest myself."

"Loaded?" Penny grinned. "Everything's ironed and ready to go." She unfolded the quilt top and shook it out. "The Christmas Glory Quilt. It really is beautiful. I can't believe it turned out so well!"

"It is pretty," her aunt said. "I never would've thought of adding red, but it makes all the difference. You have a good eye for this. We need the backing first."

"Okay." Penny relaxed as Violet explained and demonstrated. It was a good day. Outside, finally, it was winter. Puffy snowflakes fell without darkening the sky, already drifting into little clusters on the shrubbery.

"I feel like I'm getting caught up on things." Penny accepted her end of the backing fabric and started pinning it to the roller. "I don't think I was ever actually behind, but it's been overwhelming."

"You finished your first dress here. Are you going to show it to me?"

"I steamed it this morning," Penny said. "Remind me to show you later. I think you'll be surprised."

"I'm sure it's beautiful. It's for the girl who's marrying your old beau? How do you feel about that?"

"I don't know." Penny didn't even try to resist her aunt's gentle interrogation. "I don't have any feelings for John. Nothing positive, anyhow. I'd feel sorry for Dani, but I think she knows what she's getting into. The thing is, she never talks about marriage. It's all about the wedding. She'd never even mentioned John's last name until Catherine came. I don't know if she loves him or just wants a wedding and husband."

"You said it was a show." Violet shook her head.

"She's really very nice, but… maybe a little shallow. Flaky. They'll probably be very happy together." She dropped a spare pin into the magnetic dish. "I'm not going to think about them today. Did I tell you I was meeting with Brittany today? She's amazing. Maybe that's why I'm feeling so good. I didn't even have to tell her what to do. She already had it all worked up, and I just approved it. Liam will be so happy."

"She's the one who wants a White Christmas wedding?"

Penny nodded. "I've been working on the Santa Lucia costumes, too, so those two songs are permanently stuck in my head. Christmas is coming so fast. It's overwhelming."

"It's a big change for both of us," Violet agreed. "In just a few weeks, we'll both be living alone, for the first time ever. That would be a big deal even if you weren't also opening a business at the same time."

Penny sat back on her heels. "Speaking of which… Did you really invite Eleanor to live with you? That's not living alone."

"It's just temporary. I'll be going to Florida in February, so the annex will be empty. She might as well stay there until she finds a place of her own."

"It'll be nice to have her around," Penny said, "but I thought you wanted to be alone."

"It's temporary," her aunt repeated. "She'll be a guest. Now that I have my own home, I can have guests if I want to."

"She could have stayed with me."

Violet shook her head. "You're going to have your hands full, opening the shop and moving into your apartment. This way, she won't have to go through the shop every time she wants to come or go."

"That's true. I just hope my apartment's livable by the first. Jeffrey's been painting. He and Brian lugged appliances up the stairs the other day. I didn't actually hear any bad words, but I couldn't guarantee they weren't thinking them. It's a narrow staircase."

"Brian's still around, helping? I thought he was going to work on his own house for a while."

"Me, too, but he didn't." Penny eyed her aunt. "Aunt Violet, how far in advance do you make your family quilt blocks?"

"In advance? I make them as things happen. Sometimes I can't keep up and I get behind, but usually I stay on top of them." She adjusted the edge of the batting and resumed pinning. "I only have so many years left, and I need to get my share of the family history quilts done before I go Home."

It took Penny a few seconds to hear the capital H. "Well, hopefully that won't be for a long time yet. After all, we have a lot of family."

26

"Ho, Ho, Ho!"

Penny ran to the front window and looked out to see Liam carrying a large box over his shoulder. Elvis Presley Christmas music blared from the SUV's speakers, overpowering the instrumental carols she listened to as she painted.

She pushed the window open and leaned out. "Good afternoon! You look festive."

He looked up. "But soft—what light from yonder window breaks?"

Penny scooped a handful of snow from the windowsill and tossed it at him.

"Hey, that's no way to treat someone who brings you a Christmas present!"

"I'll be right down." She slid a plastic bag over the paintbrush and ran down the stairs, making a detour through the fitting room to check her reflection for paint smears.

Liam was already inside, pulling off his wool coat. Snowflakes dotted his dark hair and eyebrows. He grinned. "It's beginning to look a lot like Christmas!"

"It's only the sixth!"

"And it's about to look a lot more like Christmas." He pulled out a pocketknife and cut open the box, tilting it so Penny could see inside.

"Is that a Christmas tree? For here?" She looked up at him, delighted. "Thank you!"

"Do you have time to put it up now?"

"Yes, this is a good time. Let me go close up the paint can, and I'll be right back. Let's put it in the consultation area." She threw the last few words over her shoulder as she entered the kitchen and walked into Brian.

He rocked back and hit his head on the corner of the wall. "Ow!" Brian massaged his scalp with two fingers. "You know, Penny, if I didn't know better, I'd think you don't like me."

"Oh, Brian, I'm sorry! Are you okay?"

He examined his fingers. "No blood. Probably just a little concussion or traumatic brain injury. What's your hurry?"

"Let me see your head." She turned him around and parted his hair, but he pulled away.

"No, I'm fine. It was just a bump. I wanted to show you what I did in the garden."

She glanced out the window to the snow-covered yard. "Plant roses?"

He reached for the door handle as Jingle Bells erupted from the consultation room. Penny jumped. "Hold on. I need to go close up my paint can. Be right back."

The kitchen was empty when she returned, and she found him lounging against a wall in the consultation area, watching Liam assemble the Christmas tree.

"It's prelit," Brian informed her.

"Aren't they all, these days?" Liam asked. "I

brought some ornaments, but I didn't know what you'd want. The Chamber had a lot of garland left over, too, so I brought that to wrap around something. Maybe the porch or handrails on the steps."

He shoved the last piece into the pole and began spreading the branches. Penny started on the other side. Brian slid onto a chair and watched.

"You missed one." He nodded.

"Thanks." Liam adjusted the branch. "It's bigger than I realized it would be."

"I think it's just right!" Penny stepped back to admire the tree. "I only wish I had more people coming to see it. I don't have many clients coming between now and Christmas."

Liam stopped what he was doing and pointed at her. "This tree will make you happy. You are a happier businesswoman, you look confident and attract clients. You put more positive energy into your business, you succeed. Even if no one ever sees this tree but you, it's an asset." He went back to shaping the branches. "If it wasn't a gift, it would be a tax-deductible business expense."

"Positive energy?"

Penny ignored Brian's comment. "I hope some people get to see it. I should get some kind of speaker system for music, not just Christmas. It felt really quiet in here when I was working with Dani. Some background noise is good."

"Are you ready?" Liam plugged in the cord and the tree lit up.

"Beautiful! It's perfect. Thank you, Liam."

The gray house and blue door looked beautiful in the snow. Penny took a minute to enjoy the scene. She'd left the Christmas tree lights on, and she could see them twinkling inside. It was a lovely tree, perfect and elegant, with gold and blue glass ornaments.

She gathered up the stack of pattern books and walked carefully up the stairs. The box of garland was still on the porch. Maybe she could get to that later. Penny hummed Joy to the World as she entered the house. She touched the tree in passing. It might be just a tad glamorous for her country chic decor. She'd have to look for some rustic ornaments to tuck in among the shiny ones.

Penny dropped a pod into the coffeemaker and waited for the machine to work its magic. It would be like this when she lived here. She could come downstairs early in the morning to make coffee and sit on the patio for devotions before clients arrived. She'd never realized how many birds there were. Mornings would be a good time with birdsong and a garden.

Penny grabbed her coffee, opened the back door, and stopped. A fir tree, planted in a barrel, stood in the center of the yard. It was wound with garlands of popcorn and cranberries. Suet balls, trimmed with plaid ribbons, hung from the branches along with some kind of lumpy ornaments she couldn't identify. She stepped closer and recognized them as the ornaments Sadie and Angel had made last week, smearing peanut butter on mandarins and rolling them in mixed seeds and raisins.

Brian. He'd tried to show her last night, and she'd been too excited about Liam's tree. The big, artificial, elegant tree that was supposed to make her a successful businesswoman. She wanted to be successful.

Penny touched one of the peanut butter ornaments. They weren't sticky, in the cold air, but their sweet, earthy fragrance emphasized the reality of this tree. It was like Brian—real and sweet. She smiled as she turned to go back inside. There was nothing artificial or shiny about Brian. He was just... true. A real man.

She paused to look back at the tree before reentering the kitchen. Already, the birds had resumed their chatter and inspection of their very own Christmas tree.

27

I was going to write you a letter, but I decided I should call. Not because of your dyslexia," Dani said quickly, "but because it's the right thing to do. Did you get my check?"

"Yes, thank you. I told you you could bring it when you pick up the dress." Getting it in the mail had been better, though, without anyone to witness her kissing the check and doing an impromptu happy dance.

"The thing is, I don't need it. I don't want it."

"What? You don't need the dress?" Penny switched the phone to her other ear.

"Nope!" Dani giggled—or maybe it was hiccups. "I already got married. We eloped!"

"Eloped?" John must really be in love if Dani had convinced him to elope instead of waiting for the formal event.

"We flew to Las Vegas!"

"Las Vegas!" Penny stopped in her tracks, clutching the phone. John Trandle might be in love, and Dani may have persuaded him to elope, but there was no way he would've done it in Las Vegas. "Stop. Are you serious? You really eloped to Las Vegas?"

"Yes! With Liam!" The name came out in a squeal.

Penny dropped the phone. She could still hear Dani's excited voice as she scrabbled for it in the frozen leaves.

"Wait!" She interrupted the recital of Liam's virtues. "What happened? I mean… you eloped with Liam?" She managed to refrain from asking 'what about John?'.

"I know it was wrong of me to run off after the invitations had already been sent out, but it would've been worse to wait any longer or get a divorce later. I love Liam, and he loves me."

Penny pushed the door shut against the wind and shrugged out of her coat, listening to Dani's rapturous description of their wedding. When she paused for breath, Penny said, "I'll return your money."

"No! I want you to keep it. If it wasn't for you, I'd never have met Liam!"

"Actually, you met me when Liam introduced us." Penny dropped her purse and tote bag on the floor. "Thanks for letting me know."

"Penny, please keep the money! And the dress."

Her first official contract, and it had fallen through. Penny wanted to hang up and cry. Her offer to return the money had been a foolish reaction. She needed the money. She hardened her heart against the distress in Dani's voice. "No, it's your dress." Her policies had never been tested before, but this one was simple. The dress was Dani's, and the money was Penny's. "I'll have it delivered to your house tomorrow."

After a few beats of silence, Dani said, "Penny, you should wear that dress. You may have fitted it on me, and I love it, but that's your dress. You designed it for yourself. I bet it fits." She rushed on before Penny could interrupt. "It was your dream dress. I knew it when I asked you to make it for me. You should wear it."

Penny walked to where the gown hung on its satin hanger. It didn't drape or sway and flow as it did on a person. It just drooped, inanimate. But she knew what it would look like alive—or rather, with a living bride inside of it.

She held the phone a few inches from her ear as Dani went on, insisting on both paying for the dress and giving it to Penny.

The dress looked incomplete with its matching sash. It should be green. The bouquet should be a posy of vintage-looking roses and springy bits, with plenty of greenery. She'd pictured a pearl necklace at one time, but that didn't seem right. A silver chain, maybe.

"No!" Penny outshouted Dani. "Please stop by when you get back in town, Dani. I'll return your money or give you the gown. It was custom designed and created for you. And your veil with the clip."

Subdued, Dani spoke more quietly. "You made it for me, but it was designed for you. If I get it, I'll sell it, and then some stranger will wear it."

Penny stilled. Why did that seem so wrong? The dress belonged to Dani, and she had the right to dispose of it as she chose, but Penny Anderson Designs wasn't supposed to work like that. She created a unique gown for each bride, and having another bride wear this one wouldn't be right. It might not fit properly or suit her personality. It would probably need alterations, and what if they weren't done well? If it wasn't perfect and the bride told everyone it was a Penny Anderson Design, it would damage Penny's reputation.

"Look, when Liam and I get back, we'll come see you. Just a minute."

Penny heard Liam in the background, interrupting his wife. Rude.

Dani returned. "Liam says he has an appointment with you next week and he'll talk to you then."

Penny rolled her eyes at the complacency in her friend's voice. What happened to the confident woman she'd talked to a few months ago? Did all brides' brains turn to mush after the wedding?

"That would be fine. Tell him I'll see him next Tuesday at two."

"We're staying here until Friday and then going to see Liam's parents."

Penny tapped the button to end the conversation and then realized she'd cut off Dani's honeymoon plans. Too bad.

She paused at the sound of voices in the entryway. Did she want to talk about it? She could call Faith, but she didn't need to pour out her heart to her friend. This was a business matter, right? A client had canceled her dress order after the dress was finished. A runaway bride had backed out of her contract. Penny should resent that, not want to cry about it.

"Is something wrong?" Violet stopped in the doorway. "You look like you just saw a ghost."

"What's the matter?" Brian didn't push the older woman aside; he just moved around her and strode ahead of her into the consultation area.

"You made your dress!" Violet raised a hand to her

chest. "It's just like you drew out all those years ago."

"Mine had a green sash."

"You made your wedding dress and saw a ghost? Why did you make your dress now?"

Penny blinked at Brian's questions and refocused.

"No, I didn't. I made it for Dani Lorris. That's the girl who's getting married on New Year's Eve, to John Trandle. But she's not. She... she just married Liam."

"Married Liam? Your business adviser?" Aunt Violet sat down. "I hope she's not expecting a refund."

"They eloped. Went to Las Vegas."

Brian frowned. "With Liam? That's a bit of a shock."

He didn't look shocked. He looked angry, his head bent slightly forward like a bull.

"You didn't have any suspicion?" Violet asked. "How'd you find out?"

"She just called." Penny held up the phone. "She doesn't want a refund, and she doesn't want her dress. She wants me to have it."

"She wants you to have the dress in which she was going to marry your ex-boyfriend, because she just eloped with the guy you're seeing now." Brian spaced the words as if working out a puzzle.

Penny stared at him. "Liam's not my... we aren't... weren't interested in each other. Not that way. Obviously!"

"Sure looked like it to me."

"You thought I was interested in him? Romantically?"

"You have a track record of dating losers. I thought

Liam was an improvement."

"What?" Outraged, Penny stepped closer to him. "I don't date losers. How could you say that?"

He held up his hands to tick items off a list, and she swatted them. "I can't believe you said that."

He grabbed her wrists. "I'm sorry. That was way out of line. I just thought you'd found a good guy, and you seemed happy."

Penny jerked free. "Dating losers. Thanks a lot."

"Don't grab her like that!"

Brian staggered as Aunt Violet's cane slapped the back of his knees.

"That was a very inappropriate and hurtful thing to say." She scolded him like a child. "It was mean. You apologize to her."

"I do!" Brian started to reach for Penny and dropped his arms. "I shouldn't have said that. But you and Liam had so much in common, and you seemed to like him. You were happy. Whenever you met with him, you seemed… energized."

"I did like him! He helped me. He encouraged me to grow my business." She looked into his intent gray gaze. "Did you really think that?"

Brian turned and left the room.

"Why do you always cry on Santa Lucia Day?" Penny squeezed her mom's shoulders. "It's supposed to be a happy day. Look—Saint Adrienne Lucia, Queen of Light, bringing the light and warmth back into the winter world just like the Son of God will bring Light and Hope when He returns."

Constance leaned against her daughter. "I don't know. I just do. Maybe it's because it's a family tradition, and I'm afraid it will end with us. And it's important. Look at these people. This little parade is a scene straight from their own childhoods. They probably did it themselves. They know the songs. In every nursing home, even here in memory care, they can sing Santa Lucia and all the Christmas carols. Maybe it won't matter that the traditions die out in our generation, but I don't want them to die as long as these people are still alive to be blessed."

At a loss for a better response, Penny pointed. "Look at Uncle Olof. Violet told him these are all his nieces and nephews, and he's so proud."

"He took all of Sarah's saffron buns and put them in that little bag on his wheelchair. He keeps calling her Violet."

"Maybe she reminds him of Aunt Violet at that age," Penny said. "Do we need more saffron buns? There are still a lot of them in the car. Gingerbread, too."

"Not here," Constance said, "but we'll need them at the next stop. Can you go separate those boys, please?"

Penny redistributed the Star Children and watched Adrienne serve coffee to Uncle Olof. Aunt Violet took it for him and held it while he picked out a piece of gingerbread. Adrienne smiled graciously before moving on to the next person. Penny had been the Santa Lucia, long before her mother had grown their simple pageant into a well-orchestrated, all-day ministry.

"What are you smiling at?"

Penny jumped. "Hi, Brian! I didn't expect to see you here." She matched his friendly tone, glad to leave Tuesday's quarrel behind. She didn't want to be at odds with Brian.

He nodded toward the piano. "Ruth's playing the piano, and Hannah wanted to bring her harp. I'm the official Santa Lucia Harp Hauler."

"I'm glad they came. All your family are so musically gifted, and the Christmas sing-along is a big deal here." Penny laughed. "The aides were saying the residents don't care much for concerts unless they can sing along."

He leaned close and whispered. "I feel the same way."

Even as she chuckled, a shiver ran through her at the warmth of his breath on her neck. In some strange way, their short argument had cleared away all the remaining childish bits and pieces. Their lifelong friendship was mature now, a foundation for something new. It was a foundation God had laid and built upon.

Penny tried to recall what they'd been discussing. Sing-alongs. "The residents seem to enjoy it. Mom says most of them probably grew up with the tradition."

"I always wanted to be a Star Boy," Brian said.

"You did? Mom has to bribe the boys with large amounts of cookies and candy. I think she gave Jeffrey cash, too, the last few years he did it."

"Mom said it was a pagan festival."

Penny tipped her head, considering. "It's not pagan. It's creepy, and… well, not pagan, anyhow. We like to think of it as a cultural heritage sort of tradition.

The girls like the white robes and wreaths, and the boys like the candy. Adrienne's really good at it. She treats it as a theatrical performance. I don't think I was very good. I remember tripping on my dress and spilling coffee and all the cookies. I think Mom was glad when I retired and let Lisa do it."

"You have two of my favorite cookies—the saffron buns and gingerbread." He flagged down a passing Star Boy and got one of each. "Did you make these?"

"No, not this year. I've been so busy at the shop. I'll be there for the rosettes and krumkake next week."

"Sandbakkels, lefse, and the whole *julbord*." Brian bit into the gingerbread. "You Swedes know how to do Christmas."

"And rice porridge and herring," Penny said. "Don't forget the herring."

28

Violet

Violet set a cup of coffee in front of Brian. She didn't know if he drank coffee, but it was the thing to do with visitors. "I'm not moved in yet, but you're my first official guest."

"I'm glad to be here." He eyed the plate of sandbakkels with pleasure. "Nobody makes those like you do, Violet. Do you have a secret family recipe?"

"It's the same recipe everyone else has. I've just been making them a long time. Help yourself."

He promptly took two of them, setting one on his plate and biting into the other. "Is it okay if I make yummy noises?"

"It's nice to see someone enjoy their food," Violet said, "as long as you don't chew with your mouth open."

"My mom raised me to have good manners. Thanks."

She waited until his mouth was full. "When are you going to stop shillyshallying around and propose to my niece?"

Number one rule of verbal combat: put the opponent at an embarrassing disadvantage. It wasn't nice, but elderly women had so few tactical advantages against young people. She'd been called 'Sweetie' by a thirty-year-old cashier yesterday. Violet enjoyed watching Brian spit out a few crumbs of his cookie. She'd succeeded in catching him off-guard.

He chewed fast, so he could swallow the rest of it. "Propose to Penny?"

"Don't you think it's about time? I don't know why you young people wait so long. She's nearly thirty!"

"She's only twenty-six!"

Violet ignored that. "You've got a good job, and if she wants to continue her shop after the babies come, it will work out just fine."

"Babies."

Violet rapped the table. "Don't chew with your mouth open."

"I wasn't chewing!" He took a sip of the coffee and set the cup down, glancing at the sugar bowl before returning to her question. "What makes you think she'd marry me? Lately, it seems like she's avoiding me."

Violet smiled indulgently. Boys were so blind. "You hurt her feelings, and then you disappeared. What do you expect?"

"What do you mean I disappeared? I've been here nearly every day."

"No, I mean when you went away to college." She sipped her coffee.

"That wasn't disappearing," Brian protested. "I was at school. Penny knew exactly where I was, and I saw her when I came home on breaks, until she went away to school herself."

He hadn't touched the other cookies. This was a

man in love.

"To Penny, it looked like you disappeared. You left without declaring yourself."

He gave a rough laugh. "Declaring myself? I think that's exactly what I did wrong."

"You told Penny you were interested in her?" Violet didn't believe it. Penny had been quiet after Brian left—not hiding a secret romance, but sad and confused.

"No, you're right. I should have told her."

"Yes, you should have. So?"

"So what? Do you really think she'd welcome a proposal from me? Do you think she loves me that way—like a husband? Not like a big brother?"

Violet snorted. "You have no idea how a girl thinks of her big brother. I had two of them, and a bunch of younger ones, and I assure you, that is not how Penny thinks of you. Maybe when you were children, but it's been a long time since she thought of you as a brother."

"She doesn't look at me like she looks at Liam."

"And she doesn't look at Liam like she looks at you," Violet snapped. She picked up her coffee cup and set it down again. "Are you or are you not going to marry Penny?"

"Yes! I want to, but I'm not convinced she wants to marry me."

"She wants to marry you." Violet rose to get the percolator. "Are you ready for more coffee?"

"No, thank you." Brian placed his hand over his cup.

She filled her own and returned the percolator to the stove. Maybe she was moving too fast for him. She would have expected an engineer's thought processes to be sharper.

He waited for her to be seated. "Penny and I are friends. I tried to make it more than that, a few weeks ago, and I don't know what happened. I told her how I felt, and she avoided me until I went back to just being a friend again."

"You asked her to marry you?"

"No, not in so many words." Brian took a bite of his cookie. "I didn't want to rush her."

"Rush her?" Violet fought back the urge to grasp his shoulders and shake him.

"Well, what if she really does just think of me as a friend? If I push her, I lose her as a friend, too."

"Oh, for goodness sake. You're afraid to ask her."

"Maybe it's time."

"Have you bought a ring yet?"

Her question seemed to annoy him.

"No, since I only decided thirty seconds ago, I haven't bought a ring yet. I will, and I'll propose. If she says no, or if she laughs at me, I'm blaming you."

She ignored that. "I have something else in mind. Wait here."

Brian had consumed another cookie by the time she returned. His eyes widened as she set the box on the table between them. She'd cleaned it carefully, and even taken some linseed oil to it, but it still looked old. Not antique… just old.

"That's the box we dug up?"

"Yes. And I haven't told anyone else what's in here. I decided Penny should have it. It was a gift from a man in love to his fiancée." Violet wagged a finger at him. "A man who thought his young lady saw him as a friend. There was a letter in there. She'd saved it."

Violet handed him the transcript she'd typed up. "Would you like some water to drink?"

"Yes, please."

She occupied herself in the kitchen until Brian finished reading. She handed him his water and sat.

Brian pointed at the signature. "Was that your ancestor?"

"My father." Violet felt a wave of sadness. "And my mother. She died when I was born."

Brian looked at the table and swallowed. Emotion, not cookies. He'd finished those.

The jeweler had wrapped the polished crown in white satin. Violet lifted it from the box and opened the layers of fabric.

She heard Brian inhale as she set the small crown on the table. It gleamed under the kitchen light.

"It's called a *brudkrona*—a bridal crown. Every village church had one. Even the smallest, poorest district might have a beautiful and valuable *brudkrona*." Violet touched the crown. "Back then, the law considered betrothal to be almost the same as marriage, but of course the church didn't agree. They wanted the young people to be married, not living in sin. Some of them still went out and set up house without being married, like people do today, but if a girl was willing to wait and be married in the church, she got to wear the *brudkrona*."

Her eyes strayed back to the letter. "My mother was just a young girl when she left Sweden, but old enough to have seen other girls married in the crown and dream about wearing it herself someday. Instead, she came to America."

"That's amazing." Brian reached out a hand. "Can I hold it?"

Violet nodded. Now that the time had come, she was ready to let it go. Her father had said it would be for their daughters, and that hadn't happened, but he'd probably be glad to see it worn by his great-granddaughters.

"It's a loan," she said quickly. "Any of the Anderson girls can use it, and your own children and grandchildren."

"I'm not even married yet," Brian said. "But thank you." He picked it up and turned it over. It looked fragile and delicate in his big hands, too small to perch on a girl's head. "Is this to jab through her hair, to hold it in place?"

Violet chuckled. "Yes, to jab through her hair. Back then, a bride would have had long hair. She'd wear it loose for her wedding, but she'd braid some of it at the top, to keep the crown in place. A modern bride might use bobby pins. If they know what bobby pins are, these days."

He nodded, but she doubted he heard her. "And you think I should propose with this?"

"It would be romantic. You can give her the box and read her the letter, and then tell her you feel the same way as her great grandfather. Then go down on one knee and propose to her."

"You don't think I should have a ring?" Brian was smiling.

Violet considered. "You could do that if you want to. It's a traditional thing to do, and Penny would probably like it. You can decide if you want to tell her who the letter is from before or after you propose. But read the letter first, so she understands what it is."

"Yes, Ma'am."

He was teasing her. Violet felt herself blush, even at 83 years old. "You can do it however you like, of course. It just seems so romantic to share this moment with that sense of family history and ancestors who loved each other so much."

"Okay," Brian said. "I will. Thank you." He stood up and walked around the table to hug her. "Thank you for sharing that with me."

When he left, Violet rose and carried the dishes to the sink. Her window overlooked the back yard, where the view used to stretch out to include the river. Her mother had that view, too. She probably thought her life was secure, with her husband and children on the farm, anticipating generations of daughters and granddaughters marrying in her bridal crown. Instead, she died, and the trees grew up to obscure the river. Johannes went on, caring for the farm and raising their children, but the light went out of his world.

29

Excitement buzzed through her, and it was hard not to giggle. So many changes, so suddenly, left her unsettled, but this was an excellent thing: on Christmas Eve, she'd been free to accept the Franklins' invitation.

Penny avoided looking at Brian as Faith shook out her napkin and spread it on her lap. Like a gracious hostess, she extended her hands to initiate the prayer, but with a rather-too-theatrical exclamation, she jerked them back.

"Oh, I forgot the bread. Brian, will you get it please?" Faith smiled warmly at her brother. "There are potholders in the drawer next to the stove."

"Sure." Brian slid his chair back. "It's not Christmas dinner without the dinner rolls to mop up the gravy."

Angel pressed a hand over her mouth as soon as he left the room, her whole body shaking with suppressed glee. Faith never had been able to keep a straight face, and Penny couldn't help laughing in response to her friend's mirth. Jim rolled his eyes and caught his daughter's arm to prevent her from sliding off her chair.

"There was only one roll in there. I'm eating it." Brian emerged from the kitchen, carrying a plate and apparently oblivious to their hilarity.

Faith sagged. "Brian! That's not a roll."

He took a bite of it and spoke with his mouth full. "Tastes like a roll. It's good."

"Uncle Brian!"

He ignored his niece's exasperation and ran his finger through the icing. "Yep, this is one of the best rolls I've ever had. I especially like this white frosting that makes an X on the top. A hot cross roll." A broad grin creased his face. "It's a bun. You have a bun in the oven." He leaned down to hug his sister. "Congratulations, Faith." He clapped Jim on the shoulder as he returned to his chair. "That was really clever. Maybe this one will be a boy, so you can name him after me."

"Or a girl, and they can name her after me." Penny said.

"Or split twins." Brian finished the bun and licked his fingers.

"I want a sister," Angel insisted. "I haven't decided on her name yet. She'll be here in May, so Mom says she'll be fun by next Christmas."

"May! That's not far away." Brian glanced at Faith's midsection. "I had no idea."

"We didn't want to announce it until we were sure. The doctor says everything should be fine this time." Faith glanced at her husband. "I didn't want to tell everyone and then lose the baby again."

"A toast!" Brian held up his water goblet. "To a safe arrival for little Brian or Penelope!"

Penny sat cross-legged on the floor, enjoying the warmth of the gas fire. She'd never watched another family celebrate Christmas before. This was a good one. Angel, giddy with Christmas and sisterhood, squealed and jumped up to distribute hugs after every gift. Faith and Jim held hands. Next year, finally, there would be another child joining in the excitement.

"It's Penny's turn," Brian announced. "Hand me that green bag over there, Angel."

"But I didn't get you anything! That's not fair."

"It's a gift," Angel said. "Gifts aren't a contest."

"Thank you, Angel." Brian handed the bag to Penny and dropped down beside her.

She lifted the glossy bag, weighing it. "Hmm...." She shook it gently. "Doesn't rattle." Penny smiled up at Brian and caught him looking at her. His gray eyes met her gaze and held it. She couldn't look away—didn't want to. There were answers in his eyes.

"Do you want me to open it for you?" Angel's loud question broke the intimate connection.

"I've got it." Penny glanced down the bag and back at Brian. He was still watching her. "Thank you."

"You don't know what it is yet. Here." Brian took the bag and held it out to her. His expression—humorous, tender, and something stronger—distracted her. It was the same face, same eyes, same man... was she the one who had changed?

Penny groped through the tissue and wrapped her hand around the gift. Fresh delight flowed over her, and she pulled it out. "Thank you! It's beautiful!"

"Is it a horse?" Angel asked.

"It's a Dala horse," Penny said "I love it."

"I know you like the blue ones better than the red," Brian said. "You'll have to thank Faith for the fancy painting."

"You made this?" Penny turned the horse, examining it closely. "I didn't know you could carve."

"The Dala horse is pretty simple. The carving's the easy part." He nodded at it. "I tried to paint it, but I made a mess of it, so I gave it a fresh coat of blue paint and handed it off to Faith to finish."

"And he paid me for my time," Faith said, "because he wanted it to be from him and not both of us."

"It's perfect." Penny reached over to give Brian a hug. He reached an arm around her and drew her to his side. She stayed, setting the horse on the floor in front of her, admiring its smooth lines and rosemaling.

"Can I open another present now?"

At her daughter's question, Faith walked to the Christmas tree and pulled out a rectangular box. "It's time for this one now."

Angel sighed. "Already?"

"Yep," her dad said. "We've got a full day ahead of us tomorrow, at your grandparents' house. Open that gift and prepare to be amazed."

Angel giggled. "I'm sure it's really cute pajamas. I wonder what the book is."

"Stinker."

Jim pretended to take the box back, and Angel grabbed it. She tore open the paper and withdrew pink plaid pajamas. "And a book! Surprise!" She scrambled to her feet and made a circuit of the room, hugging everyone again. "Just think, next year you can hug my little sister goodnight, too!"

"Sadie will get her white Christmas! She's excited to try out the snowshoes she's getting." Penny tilted her head back, letting the snow fall on her face.

"She knows what she's getting for Christmas?"

"Yes, we started doing that a few years ago. Instead of a lot of small gifts, we each get one big one. A special one, that we really want. We do more for birthdays."

"That's a good way to do it. Hold on—I'll be right back." Brian went back inside and came out with a large duffel bag, pulling the door shut behind him. "It sounds like things are changing over at your house."

"It's different," Penny said, "but it makes sense. Everyone's getting married and leaving home. You know we'll still be cramming in every Swedish tradition Mom can come up with, but we're doing it all on Christmas Day instead of spreading it over two days. I think it's a good idea."

"So, you can all do your own thing on Christmas Eve." He took her mittened hand. She didn't pull away. "Want to go for a walk?"

"In the dark, in the snow?"

"Come on, Minnesota girl. Don't be a baby."

She smiled up at him. "Well, I did wear my warmest boots and mittens."

"So, you were expecting me to ask you to go for a

walk." Brian slung the bag over his shoulder.

"It's a nice night for a walk."

"Dark and snowing?" he teased.

"Snowing anyhow. It's never quite dark when it's snowing." Penny stuck out her tongue to catch flakes. "It's not even that cold."

She didn't know if it was cold or not. A shiver of excitement kept her warm inside. Anticipation. Christmas Eve, snow, Brian, after all these years. They walked in friendly silence along the empty sidewalks, stopping occasionally to admire Christmas displays. Christmas trees sparkled in nearly every front window. Organ music poured from inside the Catholic church. The splendid building was lit from within, the stained-glass windows brilliant.

Brian kept walking, and Penny began to wonder if she'd been mistaken.

"Where are we going?"

"I thought we'd go to the park. Maybe sit on a bench and watch the snowflakes cover the ice rink." He looked down at her with a smile. "Unless you want to go ice skating."

She shook her head. "Not tonight."

Brian led her through the deepening snow in the empty park. "Here." He dropped the duffel bag and brushed the snow off a bench.

Penny watched, delighted, as he pulled a blanket from the bag and draped it over the bench.

"Milady." He waved an invitation for her to sit.

"Thank you." She complied, watching his face.

After a few seconds, he grinned. "Not a surprise."

Brian dropped to one knee, in the snow, and Penny burst into tears.

He clambered to his feet and sat next to her. "Oh, Penny, if you don't want me..."

"No, no. I mean, go on." Penny shoved, and he slid back to his kneeling position, shaking his head.

"You are ruining my romantic moment. And making me even more nervous."

"Don't be nervous," Penny whispered.

Brian smiled, and she forced back another sob.

"Stop crying!" He sat back and looked at her with something that might have been exasperation but looked more like worry.

"I'm so happy." Penny sniffed. She clasped her hands together. "I'm okay."

He knelt again, and Penny gasped in the sharp cold air when he opened a small box—so classic—and a shaft of lamplight sparked on a diamond. She pressed her clasped hands against her mouth.

"Penny, you are the most incredible woman I've ever met. You've been a light in my life since you were a little girl, full of energy and sunshine, always laughing and talking and moving and singing... you became part of my world. An important, vital part. I don't know when things changed from childhood friendship to a deeper kind of love, or if it just started from the moment we met, growing together, God building us up together right from the start, making us one in every way except marriage. I want that last step now, Penny. The beginning of the next stage of our life."

He seemed vulnerable and strong and raw, with

snowflakes frosting his eyebrows and falling between them. Penny wished she could capture the magic of this moment, to treasure every word and thought as Brian looked into her eyes and her heart swelled with joy.

"I love you, Penny. We belong together. I will do whatever I can, for every moment of the rest of my life, to serve you and love you and be your husband. I want you to be happy. I love your sunshine smile and I want to share that joy. When things aren't easy—and there will be hard times—I'll be there, and we can do anything together. We'll grow old together and be best friends forever."

Penny sniffed, but he continued, holding her eyes with his earnest gaze.

"You are the most beautiful woman in the world. You light up my world. But that's just part of it. You're kind and generous and you understand people. I don't deserve you, but I hope—I pray—that you will marry me. Will you?"

Penny tumbled off the bench to embrace him in the snow.

"Yes! Oh yes, yes, yes."

He lifted her back up to the bench and sat down next to her. She tugged off the mitten with her teeth, and he took her hand.

"I promise to love and cherish and care for you all the days God gives us together." He slid the ring onto her finger and lifted her hand to kiss it.

Penny scooted close to him and rested in his arms. "Oh, Brian, that was so beautiful and romantic. I promise I will always love you, too, and do my best to be a good wife and make you happy."

She turned her face up to look at him, inviting his kiss, anticipating it, knowing how perfect it would be as a seal of their betrothal.

"Oh, Penny." He kissed her. A tender, sweet kiss of promise. The contact was precious, almost sacred. It was a brief moment, and then he gathered her in his arms and kissed her again. She felt their hearts bonding as if at last—after a lifetime of waiting—they were both completed, each separately and as one, together. The warmth of their shared love filled her body and flowed out into their kiss.

Brian grasped her shoulders and moved a few inches—too many inches, Penny thought—back. "There's more. Something I have to show you." He didn't let her go as he reached for the duffel bag straps and dragged it to the bench, but he had to release her to dig through the bag.

Penny watched him, curled as close as she could get, feeling his warmth even through layers of winter clothing. Her eyes widened as he emerged with the wooden box.

"That's Aunt Violet's box, isn't it?"

"Yes, she gave it to me, with a full script of how to propose to you."

Penny sat upright. "She what?"

"Don't worry. I didn't think much of her plan, so I listened politely and then did it my own way. Don't forget you've already said yes. I do think you'll like this, though. She wanted me to read this to you first, because she thought her parents' romance—and it's a real love story—paralleled ours in some ways. Especially the friends to lovers theme and your great grandfather's fear that the woman he loved only thought of him as a big brother."

"A big brother? You thought that? Goop." She smiled into his gray eyes.

"Sometimes. This letter was inside the box. Listen."

He pulled her against him, and they leaned back against the bench. He wrapped one arm around her, holding her to his side, and she laid her head on his shoulder. He read the letter as if he was the writer and she his beloved bride.

When he reached the end, Penny sighed happily, nestling against him. "That's so romantic. Whenever Aunt Violet's talked about her life, it's sounded so dreary. I wonder what it was like for her to read this and know her parents had been in love."

"That's my Penny, always caring about other people's feelings." He dropped the paper and kissed the top of her head. "There's more."

"More?" She glanced at the box and caught her breath. "You mean, it's in there?"

Brian took the silver crown from the box, balancing it on his palm and shifting it so it gleamed in the light. "The *brudkrona* Johannes had made for his Hilma. Violet says she doesn't know how it ended up in the box in the garden, or even if Hilma wore it." He held it up on top of Penny's head and considered it. "I like to think she did, and it's up to you, but I hope you'll wear it when you marry—" his voice broke and he pulled her close. He finished in a rough whisper. "When you marry me."

"Brian…" Penny removed the little crown from his fingers and set it in the box. "I'll wear whatever you like. I just want to marry you. Soon."

Author's Note

I didn't know much about dyslexia when Penny first took up residence in my mind. I didn't even realize, at first, that she had dyslexia. She's smart, creative, and ambitious, and it took me a while to understand that her occasional anxiety and snarkiness were defensive behaviors.

I am deeply indebted to my friend, Charlotte Dance, for her help with this book. The research was fascinating and enlightening, but I couldn't have written about this topic without her advice. She answered my oddball questions and even read the book ahead of time, so I could make sure I was portraying Penny's challenges and strengths in a realistic light. Anything I got right should be attributed to her; anything I messed up is entirely my own fault.

To learn more about dyslexia:
> https://dyslexiaida.org
> https://www.thereadingcenter.org
> http://dyslexia.yale.edu
> http://dyslexiafoundation.org

If you enjoyed *Always and Forever*, keep reading for a sneak peek of the next book in the Glory Quilts collection.

THE Swedehearts Glory Quilt

Eleanor Neilson looked around the table at the beloved, beautiful, perfect people and wondered if she was adopted. Her parents, like reigning monarchs, smiled benevolently at their well-behaved family. Even the twins, newly promoted from highchairs, sat upright in their boosters, neatly eating moderate portions of turkey and stuffing. A perfect family of blond, blue-eyed, Minnesotan Swedes.

She hadn't come prepared to dress up for dinner, and when Soren came downstairs sporting a striped shirt and bow tie, she laughed at him. Then Zack and Laurie arrived, bearing pumpkin pies, flowers, and grandchildren. Zack's suit looked like it was made for him. Laurie wore a long corduroy skirt and ivory cashmere sweater, loosely belted around her slim middle.

Her floral scarf draped gracefully into elegant folds. If Eleanor wore that, it would collect crumbs like a bib, like a chipmunk, saving morsels to consume later. It might, however, protect her sweater from gravy stains.

"There are bound to be openings for the spring semester, not just at Westerfield but other schools in the area, too. Or you could do substitute work for a while. Eleanor!" Kathy Nielson didn't raise her voice; she just changed the pitch. "I was talking to you."

"Sorry, Mom. I did hear you. I'm going to stick it out up north for a while, though." Lather, rinse, repeat. She'd given up on explanations and discussion. Just say no and take advantage of her mother's refusal to engage in a quarrel at Thanksgiving dinner.

"You may change your mind in January, though," Soren said. "Winter up there is different from being in the city. You could get snowed in at that cabin and no one would find you for weeks."

"And that would be bad because...?"

Her brother ignored the comment and continued. "Uncle Gary will want the cabin, too, like this weekend, for hunting and fishing. You can't leave town every time he wants to have a party."

"You won't want to stay there while the cabin is full of his friends," her mother said. "And he won't want you there."

"I'll stay at his house in town, or I could probably stay with Uncle Carl and Aunt Constance. They've got a lot of room there now. Only Jeffrey, Adrienne and Sarah are still at home. Aunt Violet and Penny are moving out to the farmhouse." Eleanor rather liked the idea of a nomadic existence, but that sentiment would undermine her position. "I'll be looking for a place of my own in the spring."

"You'll be back here by then." Zack handed a napkin to his daughter. "You'd miss Tara and Tyler too much to stay away that long."

"I don't imagine they'll change much by Christmas." Cold, Eleanor, Cold. She tried again. "I probably wouldn't see them again before Christmas even if I lived here!"

"I haven't seen the Anderson cousins in years," Rob said. "Probably since Jeremy's wedding. Uncle Carl said we're welcome to come for a visit whenever we want."

Eleanor smiled gratefully at her oldest brother. "They're really nice." She turned to her mother. "Did you know I used to be afraid of him?"

"Afraid of Carl? Why on earth would you be afraid of Carl?"

"It was a long time ago, when we were on our way back from some family event. You said he didn't care about any children except his own. You were mad about it."

Kathy stared at her. "I never said any such thing."

"Yes, you did. I remember that," Rob interjected. "It was some political thing. He didn't support something you did, or you didn't support something he did. It was probably about homeschooling."

"Well, if I said that—and I don't remember it!—I didn't mean you should be afraid of him. He just sees certain things differently than we do. He has a limited view of the world, from up there in the country." In other words, they were all united in their enlightened views, and her brother was a backwoods hick.

This Thanksgiving, Eleanor was most devoutly grateful she'd been away from home over the election season.

"Anyhow, at Westerfield, you'd be able to substitute whenever you like, and you'd have a foot in the door when they hire for the new campus this summer." Kathy held up a hand to prevent interruption. "I know you want a break, but if you wait too long, you'll be set back another year. They'll have openings for every subject and grade level.

Eleanor broke off another forkful of pie. She didn't want to teach at all. She'd tried to tell her mother that, but she'd made the mistake of over-explaining it, talking too long, with not enough resolve.

"Westerfield's going to be in demand," her father said. "You'll do well to get in at the start."

"I'm going to stay up north." She hoped she didn't sound as desperate as she felt. She still had two days before she could go home. Back up north, away from her dear family.

"You won't like it up there for long," Zack said, "and you aren't getting any younger. You're going to want to be near Mom and Dad and the rest of us once you get married and have kids." He chucked Tyler under the chin. "You'd like a couple cousins, wouldn't you, fella?"

Zack and Laurie, having efficiently completed their family with only one pregnancy, had recently turned their attention to Eleanor's biological clock. They—and her other brothers and parents—had introduced her to a parade of teachers, politicians, and other suitable bachelors. She knew they meant well. They were genuinely concerned about her professional career and anxiously listening to that ticking clock. She ran a hundred miles away, and they could still hear it.

"Wouldn't it be fun if they had the same nanny?" Laurie asked.

Eleanor blinked. "The same nanny?"

"Well, when the twins are in school full-time, Ilse will be available."

"So," Eleanor said, "if I got married next month, got pregnant a few months later, had the baby and stayed home for at least a few months, that timing would work out for you?"

Laurie shook her head, not responding to the sarcasm. "Weddings take at least a year to plan, and the kids won't be in kindergarten for another two years." She sipped her coffee. "It was just a thought."

"Not to mention the fact that she doesn't have a boyfriend," Soren said, "but I suppose she could go ahead and start planning the wedding now."

"She's twenty-seven." Zack cut open a roll and spread cranberry butter on it. "She'd better start planning something."

"I don't need this." Eleanor stood, pushing her chair back. "I don't know if or when I'll get married, or if I'll have kids, but I've made one decision: I won't be returning to school in the fall. I am not going back to teaching." She almost enjoyed the moment of stunned silence. Even Tara, who'd been running a finger through the whipped cream on her pie, stopped and looked at her. "I don't know what I'm going to do, but I don't think I'm cut out to be a teacher."

"Not cut out..." Kathy Nielson's appalled voice trailed off.

"You're a good teacher," her father said. "Maybe

you should look into high school or even college. Middle school can be rough."

"No, Dad. I'm just not good at it." She gestured widely, to encompass all of them. "That's you. Just because it's what you do, doesn't mean it's for me. I'm not like you."

"What else would you do?" Her mother asked.

"I don't know." She picked up her phone from the table and stuck it in her pocket. "I need some time to think about it."

They didn't give her time. They tag-teamed her, nagging and lecturing and reasoning, until she threatened to apply for a job as a Walmart greeter.

"You're a little overqualified for that," her mother said.

"I think I'd be rather good at it."

"I hope you're joking."

"Really," Eleanor insisted. "You say hello when they come in, help them with their carts, give stickers to the kids and then wave goodbye when they leave. It sounds like the perfect job."

Her mother reached out and caught Eleanor's hands. "Sweetheart, I'm sorry we've been pressuring you, but we just want the best for you. You are a good teacher, and it's important, meaningful work. You're making a difference in the lives of children. Investing in the future of America. The world!"

Was that supposed to be encouraging? It sounded like more pressure. "I don't think I was making a difference, Mom. I never felt like I was accomplishing anything at all. The world had better not count on me."

The older woman hesitated as if approaching a delicate topic. She shifted closer, still holding Eleanor's hands, and gazed into her eyes. "Your father and I have been talking. You've been going through a hard time, and maybe you should talk to someone. We'd be happy to pay for a counselor."

"Because I don't want to be a teacher?" Eleanor stood. "Come on, Mom... there are other careers in the world!"

Her mother's tender mood evaporated. "Maybe there are, but I don't see you pursuing any of them. You've just run off to find yourself, without thinking of anyone else."

Eleanor took a step forward. "I'm sorry, Mom. I'm not a teacher."

"Oh, Eleanor."

Their embrace felt hollow, as if nothing had been mended, but it had been an embrace. She wasn't leaving in an open quarrel. Hopefully, things would be better at Christmas. Or maybe there would be a blizzard, and she'd get snowed in at the cabin.

She should have listened to her mother. Eleanor leaned forward, clutching the steering wheel as if afraid it might jerk away and throw the Subaru Outback into the ditch. She'd left early enough to get home before dark, but at four o'clock, dusk hung in the trees. At least it wasn't snowing. A gray shadow flashed in her peripheral vision, and she flinched. She hadn't hit a deer since she was 18, but she still remembered the sick feeling.

The road narrowed to a tunnel, overhung with tree boughs, pines pressing in on both sides. Soren was right; she could get snowed in here. Uncle Gary said he'd keep it plowed, but what if there was a big storm or, like last year, new snow every day? She could never shovel her way out.

Relief lightened her spirits as she passed the sign and motion-activated floodlights lit the driveway. She'd become fond of that fish-shaped sign since moving here. Its incorrectly placed apostrophe used to niggle at her, until her mother pointed out that since her brother was single, it was the proper usage. Currently single, her mother had clarified. Eleanor wondered if he kept a sign that said The Andersons' in storage for his married phases.

She pulled into the garage and shut off the engine. She couldn't stay here through the winter. She'd be a basket case by December—even worse than she'd been six months ago, when she'd finally made the decision to leave her job and set out to find herself. She'd never find herself out here. She was lucky to find the cabin.

Cabin was a misnomer. Uncle Gary didn't seem to grasp the concept. This place was larger than his house in town and more luxuriously appointed. She tapped in the security code and pushed the door open. The hallway light came on automatically, flooding the great room with comfort. Through the glass wall of windows, security lights illuminated the backyard—front yard? Eleanor wasn't used to thinking of the road access as the backyard. The front yard was the one on the lake.

She switched off the exterior lights and went into

the kitchen. In the evenings, now that it was dark so early, she felt exposed in the great room, with its massive glass wall. She preferred the interior spaces and the dining room, where blinds offered privacy from anyone skulking outside or on the lake.

Eleanor wrinkled her nose at the faint fragrance of cigar smoke. The refrigerator was probably full of beer, too, if her uncle and his friends hadn't drunk it all. He griped about city hunters who came up, drank themselves to sleep and then went out hung over, but he wasn't exactly abstinent himself. Eleanor cleared out for the long weekend, according to their agreement, so they could have their annual hunting trip. She hoped she wouldn't see deer carcasses hanging from trees in the morning.

They'd been tidy, at least. The furniture wasn't in exactly the same position she'd left it, and the mudroom was... muddy. Cleaning was her responsibility—even cleaning up after a hunting party. Free rent came with a price.

The trill of her phone, unexpected in the silence, startled her. Her mother, of course. Eleanor picked up her coat and rummaged for the phone.

"Hi, Mom. I made it safely."

"Good! I've been worried. How was the trip?"

"Uneventful—the best kind."

"No deer? Was the traffic bad?"

"It was all going in the other direction. Hunters heading home with dead deer strapped to the tops of their SUV's. I had the northbound road to myself. And it's not exactly an expedition across the country." It sure felt like it, for the last 20 miles, though. Eleanor rolled the stiffness from her neck.

"Far enough, during hunting season, in the dark."

True. "Well, I just got here and dropped my bag in the hall. I'm going to put your care package in the fridge and get unpacked. I have work in the morning." She could hear her mother's disapproval in the brief silence. "It was fun to spend Thanksgiving with all of you. Tell Dad I love him and I'll beat him at chess when I'm there for Christmas."

"That reminds me." Her mother ignored Eleanor's attempt to end the conversation. "After you left, we started talking about our anniversary. Laurie wants to have a party for us."

"On Valentine's Day?"

"The fifteenth. Valentine's Day is on a Thursday. It was all her idea, but your dad and I are looking forward to it."

Her sister-in-law had jumped right into the Nielson family, not only adding another female to their male-dominated family but producing grandchildren. Twins. Laurie was an overachiever. Eleanor, still single with no prospects in sight, was a failure in more ways than one. It hadn't even occurred to her to throw a party. She would have called, of course, and maybe even remembered to send a card.

"That will be nice! I'll be there." They all knew she didn't have any other plans for Valentine's Day.

The Great Lakes Series

Baggage Claim

Snow Angels

Chasing Grace (Summer 2021)

Hope for the Holidays

Home Run (Spring 2022)

The Glory Quilts Series

Always and Forever

The Swedehearts Glory Quilt

Serenity Hill Series

Season of Change

Starting Now (Fall 2021)

After 40 years of wandering (but always in lovely places and not in a desert), Cathe Swanson has recently returned home to her childhood home and family in Minnesota. In the summer, she and her husband enjoy spending time with their grandchildren and being outdoors, gardening, hiking, birdwatching, and kayaking. The long winters are perfect for playing games, reading, and indoor hobbies. Cathe's been a quilter and teacher of quiltmaking for nearly 30 years and enjoys just about any kind of creative work, especially those involving fiber or paper.

Everything inspires new books! A lifelong love of quilting, Cathe's Swedish heritage and an interest in genealogy led to The Glory Quilts series, and The Great Lakes series is based on her life in the Midwest and experiences with the elderly, the military, and inner-city ministry. As a child of the 60's, she's having fun writing about hippies and the Jesus People movement in the Serenity Hill series.

Made in the USA
Monee, IL
07 October 2020

44234609R00131